"I don't want our child to grow up knowing only one of its parents," Bram insisted

This was one option Dani hadn't considered. It wouldn't be so bad, she assured herself. How long would Bram Fortune, determined ladies' man, remain interested in playing part-time daddy? Not long at all.

"I wouldn't have a problem granting paternal visitation rights."

"I have no intention of being an every-other-Saturday-afternoon-at-the-zoo kind of father, Dani."

Her stomach clenched. A headache began pounding at her temple. "What exactly are you suggesting, Bram?"

"There's only one logical way to handle this."

Dani's palms broke into a sweat. "What's that?"

"Isn't it obvious?" His answering smile was a wolfish slash of white. A predator's smile. "We have to get married."

Talented and popular **JoAnn Ross** just keeps delighting her many fans with her wonderful stories. She is the author of over fifty novels, with more than eight million copies in print, and we are delighted that JoAnn is also part of a new project with Harlequin. Mira Books is a new imprint featuring the best writers creating the best stories in women's fiction. *Legacy of Lies* will be available from Mira Books in February 1995. Look for it at your local bookstore!

Books by JoAnn Ross

SCANDALS

JoANN ROSS

Harlequin Books

TORONTO • NEW YORK • LONDON
AMSTERDAM • PARIS • SYDNEY • HAMBURG
STOCKHOLM • ATHENS • TOKYO • MILAN
MADRID • WARSAW • BUDAPEST • AUCKLAND

ISBN 0-373-25606-X

SCANDALS

Copyright © 1994 by JoAnn Ross.

1

HIS BROTHER WAS DEAD.

The thought struck as harshly as the bright California sun streaming through the cabin windows. Seconds later, the dull throbbing in Bram Fortune's head reminded him of last night.

Squeezing his eyes against the unwelcome morning light, he reached for the half-empty glass of scotch he'd left on the coffee table. Propping himself up on one elbow, he downed the twelve-year-old liquor in long, thirsty swallows.

His mouth felt as if the Creature from the Black Lagoon had spent the night wading through it. Christ, Bram thought grimly, today was going to be rough enough to get through, without having to face it with the mother of all hangovers.

Reminding himself that he'd never been known for his restraint, he poured two fingers of scotch into the now-empty glass, then, on reconsideration, added a splash more. He bent down, groping for the pack of cigarettes he vaguely remembered having dropped onto the floor.

He shook a cigarette loose, tapped it on the table, stuck it between his lips and lit it with the monogrammed, twenty-four-karat-gold lighter Eden Vail had bought him for Christmas.

As he drew the acrid smoke into his lungs, Bram considered that one of the things he liked about the voluptuous blond actress—aside from the obvious—was that she was one of the few individuals in Hollywood who wasn't on a health kick.

In the six weeks they'd been sleeping together, never, not once, had she suggested he give up his beloved scotch for designer water. And she never lectured him about secondhand smoke. That alone made her worth keeping around.

The telephone rang, reverberating through his head like a fire alarm. He snatched up the receiver. "Yeah?"

"Bram?" As if conjured up by his thoughts, Eden's melodious voice echoed across the long-distance wires. "It's me, darling. I thought you might like a wake-up call."

She knew him too well. He squinted at the Rolex wristwatch lying on the table beside the glass.

"Thanks, babe." Bram's voice was rough and gravelly. He resisted the urge to cough. "That was real thoughtful. But I've been up for hours."

"Oh." She sounded disappointed. He could practically see her ripe pink lips turning down in a seductive pout. "I thought you might have tied one on."

"Who, me?" If he'd been directing this particular script, the margin cue would have read, *Feigned innocence.*

"Well, you have had a horrendous five days, sweetheart. It wouldn't be surprising if you got a little drunk. I know if I was burying my kid brother today—"

"Thanks for the concern," he growled. The idea of Ryan dying was hard enough to take. He wasn't prepared to contemplate the idea of his baby brother being lowered into the still-frozen ground. "But I'm doing fine. Really."

"I still wish you'd let me come up there."

From the time the news about Hollywood's hottest writer-director being nearly killed while cross-country skiing in California's High Sierras with his brother had hit the wires, the media had turned the Fortune family tragedy into a three-ring circus. Bram knew that if Eden had arrived on the scene, things would have gotten even crazier.

"It's not that I wouldn't love to have you with me," he lied, lowering his voice to what he hoped was a seductive drawl. "But my family isn't used to the spotlight, babe. I'm trying to keep this as low-key as possible."

"I understand." He heard her soft sigh. A mental image of those lush, silicone-enhanced breasts that had graced the cover of last month's *Playboy,* flashed through his mind. "But I still wish there was something I could do to make you feel better."

Her signature breathy voice was tinged with sex and sin. Usually just hearing it was enough to make him hard. Today, Bram was relieved he wouldn't be required to rise to the occasion.

"Keep that thought," he said. "I'll be home in a couple of days."

"I'll be waiting," she promised. Then, just when he thought she was going to hang up, she said, "Oh, I almost forgot. Sydney called this morning."

Sydney Kohn, president of Eclipse Studios. As grim as he was feeling, Bram couldn't resist a faint, knowing smile as he realized the real reason for Eden's call.

"Oh? What did that vampire want?"

"Really, Bram," she protested, "you shouldn't call him that. Actually, Sydney was quite concerned about you."

"All that man cares about is his precious, goddamn bottom line," Bram countered brusquely. When he chose, he could be charming. When he didn't choose, he could turn white-hot. Or even more dangerous, as cold and treacherous as ice.

Ever since the studio had been sold to a Japanese computer conglomerate, financial screw-tightening had gotten worse than ever. For not the first time, Bram found himself wishing for the good old days when films were made by people who truly loved movies and whose main goal was to tell a good story.

"Let me guess. Sydney wanted to know if my brother's untimely demise, not to mention my close call with the Grim Reaper, was going to delay production on *Scandals.*"

Her slight pause spoke volumes. "Well, the subject did come up," she admitted reluctantly. "But only in passing."

She was a liar. A lovely one, but a liar just the same. And beneath her deceptive cotton-candy looks there lurked a relentless ambition. That was another one of the things Bram liked about Eden. When it came to her work, she was every bit as driven as he. And as ruthless.

"I'll just bet it did." He ground the cigarette out into the overfilled ashtray on the floor.

"Well, he did explain that things are crazy around Eclipse right now. The entire Muishito board of directors descended on him en masse, yesterday. Apparently they actually expected him to set them up with dates with movie stars."

"Sounds reasonable to me." Bram suspected he knew who one of those dates might be.

"And that religious group is having all their members write to the network, threatening a boycott of the sponsors if *Scandals* airs."

Bram's curse was vicious. The crazies had come crawling out of the woodwork as soon as it was announced that he'd agreed to write and direct the miniseries that was a joint project between Eclipse Studios and the network.

"Did Sydney happen to mention how the network feels about the boycott threat?"

"Right now, they're holding firm to air *Scandals* during the fall sweeps."

Bram wondered how long that resolve would last. Movie investors might be a nervous bunch, but they weren't nearly as gutless as the television executives he'd met.

"Which is why Sydney is worried about any delays," she added.

"Tell Sydney neither rain nor snow nor sleet, nor the death of a loved one will keep Bram Fortune from completing his appointed picture. On time. And under budget."

There was a long silence on the other end of the line. "You don't have to use that sarcastic tone with me, Bram." Bram pictured the tears welling up in those big baby blue eyes. Of all the actresses he'd ever worked with, none could weep on cue like Eden. "You know all I care about is you."

"I know, sweetheart." Even as he said the words, Bram found himself wondering just how long she'd stick around if he were any ordinary man. A plumber, perhaps. Or a truck driver. Or even a doctor like his father. And his brother.

Ryan.

The horrific sight of his baby brother, being swept away by a vast tidal wave of snow, flashed through his mind.

Bram dragged his hand through his dark hair, contemplated another drink and decided he'd better wait. His mother had been through enough. Having her surviving son show up roaring drunk at her younger son's burial would not make her day.

"Look, babe, I hate like hell to cut this short, but I've got to get ready for the services."

"All right." She sounded as eager as he to end the unsatisfactory conversation. "I'll see you soon."

"Two days."

"I'll be waiting." Another little pause. "Ah, do you want me to meet your flight? I promised Sydney I'd have lunch with Tatsuo Matsumoto," she said in a breathless little rush, "but—"

"Don't worry." Far be it from him to interfere with Eden's personal career advancement. He was vaguely surprised to discover that he wasn't the least bit jealous. "I've got to run by the studio and hold Sydney's hand, anyway."

It was definitely not his first choice. But if it took a little schmoozing to keep those Ginza suits from snatching his picture away and handing it over to some bargain-basement director, that's exactly what he'd do.

"I'll just take a car from the airport."

"If you're sure."

"Positive." He forced a smile he was a very long way from feeling into his tone. "Love ya, babe."

"I love you, too, Bram."

She was making little kissing sounds with those ridiculously sexy lips when he hung up.

Bram leaned his head against the back of the couch, closed his eyes and watched Ryan's crimson parka disappear beneath the roiling white snow.

Pain stabbed through him, slicing at his heart, twisting his gut, making his head pound. Fighting off the urge for another drink, he pushed himself to his feet.

He grimaced at the stench of stale sweat, liquor and cigarette smoke emanating from his unwashed flesh. As he made his way unsteadily to the bathroom to take a much-needed shower, guilt rode heavily on Bram Fortune's slumped shoulders.

TWO MILES AWAY, in the quaint, wooded resort town of Tahoe City, California, located on the northwest corner of America's most celebrated alpine lake, Dani Cantrell sat on the padded bedroom window seat, staring out at the white drifting snow.

Across the room, her wedding dress, a fanciful confection of ivory lace studded with seed pearls, hung on the closet door. A stark black wool dress was draped across the end of her bed.

She leaned her forehead against the cool glass and closed her eyes. But she could not block out the heart-wrenching scenes that had been running unceasingly through her mind for days.

Dani and Ryan Fortune had been best friends all of their lives. Dani's mother, who'd divorced her sculptor husband before Dani's birth, had been the Fortunes' live-in housekeeper. Dani and Ryan grew up under the same roof. As had

Ryan's brother, Bramwell. But since Bram was six years older, he'd always had his own life. His own friends.

Which had suited Dani just fine. She'd loved having Ryan all to herself. And truthfully, she'd never cared much for Bram. He was too brash, too conceited. And definitely too cocky.

Bram Fortune was, Dani thought now, the opposite side of the coin from his loving, sensitive brother. He'd also been, she admitted, too much of a challenge. From the first time she'd batted her thick ebony lashes in the cradle, Dani had realized her ability to beguile. Only Bram had proved stubbornly impervious to her feminine charms.

When they were babies, Dani and Ryan splashed side by side in the bathtub. When they were four they had chicken pox together, and shortly after they turned six, holding hands tightly to ward off innumerable, nameless fears, they walked the long block to the redbrick school for the first day in Mrs. Howard's first grade.

They ran wild in the woods, picking berries and eating more than they ever brought home, which on more than one occasion had resulted in tummy aches that Maureen Cantrell, Dani's mother, had soothed with peppermint tea.

The two best friends could not have been more different. Dani, the blithe spirit, was continually encouraging the more sober-minded Ryan to spread his wings, while Ryan managed, with varying success, to keep Dani grounded.

Ryan enjoyed Saturday afternoons tinkering with his chemistry set. Convinced that the ability to fly was merely a case of mind over matter, Dani spent one memorable summer jumping off the roof. Again and again. The fact that she never actually became airborne did not discourage her. Obviously, her belief wasn't strong enough, she'd explained to a skeptical Ryan.

One balmy August afternoon, when they were eleven, Dani realized that more than a week had gone by without an adventure. Obviously, something needed to be done. Without bothering to tell their parents, Dani and Ryan bicycled four miles north to Squaw Valley, where they rode the aerial tram to the Granite Chief restaurant situated at a dizzying elevation of 8,200 feet.

They admired the breathtaking panoramic view over cherry colas and thick gooey slices of banana-cream pie. Afterward, they rode the tram back down.

And then, blowing the last of Ryan's allowance, they made the scenic trip again.

After they'd returned home and were summarily grounded for two weeks, Ryan, always the gentleman, tried to shoulder all the blame. Dani, who, despite her carefree nature, believed in taking full responsibility for her actions, wouldn't let him.

Both agreed that the day had been worth the punishment.

Their freshman year of high school, looking wonderfully resplendent, she'd thought at the time, in a rented tuxedo with a powder blue jacket and ruffled shirt, Ryan had escorted Dani to the school's Valentine's Day dance.

Years later, Ryan would confess that Dani, dressed in a hot pink taffeta formal that rustled seductively when she walked, her first pair of high heels and natural pearl earrings borrowed from his mother, was the most beautiful sight he'd ever seen.

On that memorable evening, however, he'd been struck dumb by the sheer wonder of seeing his childhood playmate transformed into a desirable young woman.

They kissed, and although it certainly wasn't the first kiss they'd shared, both knew instantly that it was different. That they were different.

And as the night grew late and the kisses became longer and sweeter, Dani Cantrell and Ryan Fortune had also known, in that shimmering, glorious, suspended atmosphere of pure sexual awareness, that they were destined to spend the rest of their lives together.

Unfortunately, life intervened to separate the young lovers. Three years after that romantic dance, Dani moved to Oregon to study art at the University of Portland. Ryan remained behind in California, earning an undergraduate degree at Pomona College before following in his father's footsteps at U.C. Berkeley's medical school. During Ryan's years in medical school, Dani was in Europe, studying painting in Paris.

And although they continued to correspond with long, chatty letters, sharing their hopes and dreams, along with their fears, as if by unspoken mutual consent both refrained from mentioning marriage.

In Paris Dani met Peter Bannister. Heir to a California oil fortune, Peter had seemed intelligent, witty, and, to a young woman who'd grown up in California's High Sierra country, devastatingly sophisticated. He was also, amazingly, even more impulsive and fun minded than she.

He swept Dani off her feet and married her in Monte Carlo before she had time to catch her breath. Their luxurious suite at the Hotel Hermitage had boasted a dazzling view of the Mediterranean and the famed Rock of Monaco.

She'd been Peter Bannister's wife for twelve short hours the first time he hit her.

Immediately after the afternoon garden wedding, Peter had taken her to the casino where he'd tried to teach her the intricacies of baccarat. The gilded gaming rooms at the casino were like something out of the movies. As she rubbed elbows with the formally dressed Richard Gere, Cindy Crawford and Michael Douglas, Dani had felt a definite kinship with Cinderella.

To her new husband's dismay, gambling proved to hold scant interest for Dani. And, for all her avowals that an artist needed to "live on the edge," the abandon with which her new husband tossed around the five-hundred-dollar chips gave her a stomachache.

When he moved on to chemin de fer, a fast-paced, high-stakes variation of baccarat, she suggested they leave. Dani could see the scene as if it were yesterday.

"Please, Peter," she'd said earnestly, after he'd lost a mind-boggling twenty-thousand dollars in a single hand. "Let's go back to our room."

"Not now." He accepted another glass of champagne from the waitress who always seemed to be hovering nearby. Although Dani hadn't counted Peter's drinks, she knew he'd imbibed a great deal in the last four hours and suspected that might have something to do with his losing streak.

"But, Peter—"

He quaffed the champagne and snagged another glass from the silver tray. "You don't understand the etiquette of the game, Danielle. I can't leave while I'm down."

A thirty-something redhead in a gown so impossibly tight Dani had wondered how she could sit down, smiled up at Dani and said, "Your husband's right. It's bad form to leave on a losing streak."

The problem was, Dani had already determined that it was impossible to get him to leave the table when he was winning.

"Peter." She put her hand on his shoulder. "It's our honeymoon," she reminded him in a smoky voice. She batted her lashes in her best Scarlett O'Hara manner. "And I'm tired."

Anyone present would have had to be deaf to miss the sultry, gilt-edged feminine invitation in her tone.

Across the table, the dealer discreetly cleared his throat.

"You're interrupting the game." Peter's eyes were chips of blue ice. His voice was tight. "If you're tired, Dani, go to bed. I'll be along later."

With that curt dismissal, he returned his attention to his cards, leaving her feeling embarrassed and angry and abandoned.

Since the casino had lost all its charm, she walked the few steps to their hotel, where she returned to the suite and took a long, calming bath in perfumed water. Afterward, always the optimist, she smoothed lotion over her body and followed up with a dusting of scented powder. She slipped into the stunning emerald green silk nightgown she'd bought only that morning in a boutique in Palace Square and brushed her wavy, waist-length jet hair into submission.

Then she climbed into the high antique bed and waited for her husband.

She was to have a very long wait. The sun was a blinding gold ball, rising from the turquoise waters of the Mediterranean beyond the ornate balcony when Peter finally returned to the suite.

He was rumpled and unshaven. His tie was gone and his starched shirtfront was missing two ebony studs. Red veins crisscrossed the whites of his eyes like highway lines on a roadmap.

"You're back." Okay, Dani admitted, so it wasn't exactly a scintillating opening line. But after the lonely wedding night she'd suffered, she wasn't exactly feeling in top form herself.

"Now that's a pithy observation." He leaned one hand against the bedpost and looked blearily down at her. "Christ. I never realized how clever you were, Danielle."

His atypical sarcasm cut at her. "I was concerned about you."

He arched a blond brow. "Were you?"

"Of course."

He leaned down until his face was inches from hers. She could smell tobacco and cognac. And a suffocatingly sweet gardenia scent that was definitely not hers. "If you were so concerned about your husband, my darling bride, you would have stayed where you belonged."

"The cigarette smoke was giving me a headache." It was the truth. Not the whole truth, Dani admitted. But enough for now.

He behaved as if he hadn't heard her. "You should have stayed. Where you belonged. With your husband." His hands curled painfully around her bare shoulders. "Do you know how humiliating it was for me, to have my wife run off like that? On my goddamn wedding night?"

His fingers were digging into her flesh. Reminding herself that discretion was the better part of valor, Dani decided not to point out that it had been *her* wedding night, as well.

"I didn't mean to—"

"Don't argue with me, dammit!" He cut off her words with a swift, harsh, openhanded slap across her mouth. Dani sucked in a sharp breath at the salty taste of her own blood. "Don't you ever, *ever*, argue with me again. Not in private." His fingers grasped her chin, holding her shocked gaze to his. "And most particularly, not in public."

Anger and pride rose to save her, steamrollering over her fear. She pulled loose and reached for the phone.

"If you so much as lift a finger to me again, Peter Bannister," she warned on a low, tight voice, "I'll call security."

His blue eyes narrowed consideringly. "You wouldn't."

She lifted her chin and met his dare. "Try me."

He gave her another long look. Then, with a muttered curse, he turned and stalked out of the suite, slamming the door behind him.

Dani lowered her forehead to her bent knees and wondered what on earth had gotten into him.

And more important, what she had gotten herself into.

Three hours later, he returned, profusely contrite. He apologized—on bended knee!—cried copious tears and blamed his aberrational behavior on wedding jitters, his unfortunate losing streak at the tables and an excess of champagne. He also gave her a belated wedding gift—a breathtaking pair of emerald earrings set in gleaming gold.

Moved far more by his tears than the precious jewels, Dani forgave her new husband.

"That was your first mistake," she murmured now as she dragged her mind back from that fateful day. Dani combed her hands through her thick shoulder-length hair and sighed.

Her second and nearly fatal mistake had been staying in the marriage for five abusive years.

She and Peter moved to San Francisco, where he went to work in his father's oil company. Although she and Ryan had both ended up in the same city, Peter proved to be a jealous and possessive husband.

Dani's letters to her childhood sweetheart dwindled to annual Christmas cards. Then they stopped entirely.

It was easier that way.

Safer. She might never have seen Ryan again if fate hadn't stepped in. On what would become her last night in Peter Bannister's Pacific Heights mansion, she was so badly beaten that the housekeeper, who found her unconscious, had called 911.

The paramedics had rushed her to St. Francis Memorial Hospital, where Dr. Ryan Fortune coincidentally happened to be on duty in the emergency room.

For two weeks he'd hovered over Dani like an overprotective German shepherd. When she was released from the hospital, it was to Ryan's Sausalito houseboat that she went.

It was Ryan who held her hand during those humiliating interviews with the police.

"Why didn't you leave?" one young officer, who hadn't even looked old enough to vote, had asked.

To Dani's immense shame, she found she couldn't answer. How could she explain that somewhere along the way, she'd lost that same self-confidence that had enabled her to go off to Paris on her own? How could she make clear that having never failed at anything she'd ever tried—with the exception of that long-ago attempt to fly—she couldn't easily walk away from something as important as marriage?

And worst of all, how on earth could she make anyone understand how, after years of being trapped in this hellish marriage, she'd actually come to believe that she deserved Peter's abuse?

With Ryan's encouragement, Dani began counseling in order to sort out the answers to those questions. Not for the police, but for herself. And when the wealth and influence of the powerful Bannister family succeeded in keeping Peter out of jail, it had been Ryan who'd cheered on her display of temper.

Although he'd wanted Dani to stay on the houseboat with him, she moved into her own apartment, continued counseling and started to paint again—to regain control of her life.

One year after her release from the hospital, on a rainy October day, Dani's uncontested divorce was final.

That same night, in a plush leather banquette at San Francisco's famed L'Etoile restaurant, Ryan proposed. Heady with a restored sense of freedom and self-confidence regained, Dani blissfully accepted.

They set the date for Valentine's Day, in commemoration of that gloriously romantic night so many years before.

Wanting to celebrate those old feelings, they decided to marry in their hometown of Tahoe City. In Ryan's parents' front parlor. And although Maureen Cantrell had died two years earlier, Amanda Fortune, professing to be thrilled with the love match, treated Dani more like her own daughter than a prospective daughter-in-law.

In her professional life, her name had begun to garner recognition in art circles. The prices earned by her works exceeded even Dani's most hopeful expectations. As for her more important personal life, she was about to become Mrs. Ryan Fortune.

Dani could not have been happier.

Five days before the wedding, Bram—who was now an internationally renowned writer/producer/director—arrived from Los Angeles to serve as best man. It had been his idea that the brothers go cross-country skiing in the Desolation Valley Wilderness, a vast, glaciated area west of Lake Tahoe.

"It'll be just like old times," he promised his younger brother.

"Watch out for Bigfoot," Dani laughingly warned. There'd been another sighting of the mythical man-beast the week before.

Promising to watch out for any oversize hairy monsters, Ryan had swept her into his arms and surprised her by kissing her breathless right in front of his brother.

And then he was gone.

Dani had no way of knowing those would be the last words she'd ever say to him.

2

LATE THAT AFTERNOON tragedy struck.

"It began to snow," Bram had told them, after being rescued from the craggy mountain heights. "The wind had picked up, driving snow into our faces like white bullets...."

At the rescue station a frantic Dani heard Bram tell the heartbreaking tale, his voice flat and emotionless, his eyes glazed and focused on some distant, unseen horror.

"The snow was thick and wet and heavy. Our skis kept sinking into the stuff. I was in the lead. Ryan was about a hundred yards behind me. I heard a sound like a tree branch snapping."

He stopped, sucked in a deep, painful breath and dragged his hand over his face.

"Then there was a low, rumbling sound. Like a growl." Bram knew he'd never forget that next sound. "Just when I turned around to warn Ryan, the mountain exploded."

Dani began to shiver violently.

Amanda Fortune, Ryan and Bram's mother, began to sob; her husband's eyes were bright with tears.

Lost in his own nightmare, Bram closed his eyes and pressed his fingers tightly against his lids, trying to block out images too painful to remember.

"The snow was boiling, taking with it everything in its path—boulders, trees, ice." He remembered all too well the way the avalanche thunder filled the air and echoed off the ridge lines. He removed his hands from his eyes and looked straight at Dani. His dark eyes were those of a man who'd visited hell and had lived to tell about it.

"I was hit in the chest by the limb of a passing tree," he said in that same flat emotionless voice that made the hair on her arms and the back of her neck stand up.

"It knocked me out of the way and I was lying on my back when I saw a flash of red tumbling by me and realized that it was Ryan's jacket."

Amanda's sobs grew louder. Tears trailed in silent ribbons down her husband's craggy face.

"I tried to reach him, but it felt as if the ground beneath my feet had turned to wild, bucking waves. Suddenly Ryan reached out of the churning mass of snow and I managed to grab his wrist.

"But then a rock came down on my head, stunning me just long enough that I must have relaxed my grip because the next thing I knew, I was watching Ryan being swept away."

Dani heard a loud painful sob and realized it had escaped from between her own parted lips.

Bram gave her a long, unfathomable look before continuing.

"I kept my eye on his red jacket and watched him become buried beneath a mountain of snow and rocks and tree limbs. And then, finally, everything turned so still it was eerie. It reminded me of all those films they used to show us in school, about the silence after a nuclear explosion.

"I crawled to the last spot I'd seen Ryan and I dug and I dug and I dug, but I couldn't find him." Bram's broad shoulders shook, as if he were sobbing, but his eyes remained unrelentingly dry. And unfocused. "I guess you all know the rest."

They did. When the Fortune brothers failed to return home that afternoon, a search team had been organized. They found Bram, his hands frozen from his frantic search for his brother, his face snow- and wind-burned, his lips chapped and bleeding.

Volunteers from all over the state probed the area with ten-foot poles. It was a ranger from Yosemite National Park who, five days after the tragedy, finally located the frozen body.

The following day the county medical examiner, completing his autopsy, declared that Ryan Fortune had died of suffocation.

The funeral was intensely personal. Unlike other memorial services that Dani had attended, where the minister was obviously a stranger to the deceased, Father McLaughlin had known the Fortune family for years.

The priest spoke in familiar, glowing terms of the young man who'd given so much to so many during his brief time on earth.

Ryan Fortune had been a warm and loving and generous man.

Unfortunately, now he was dead.

Dani knew that eulogies weren't customary at Catholic funerals, which was why she was surprised when Father McLaughlin announced that the family had asked Bramwell Fortune to say a few words about his brother.

Bram's expression, as he left his mother's side in the front pew of the church and took his place behind the walnut lectern, was inscrutable. Dark-framed glasses with smoke-hued lenses concealed his eyes.

"Not long ago—" his deep voice filled the high-raftered church "—Ryan came down to visit me for a weekend in Los Angeles. Naturally, he stayed at my house, and on his last night in town, we sat out on my deck overlooking the moon-gilded waters of the Pacific. And as so often happens when the night grows late and the scotch begins to flow freely, internal walls came down, allowing us to talk about life. And death.

"On what I couldn't have known would turn out to be our last night together, I learned more about my brother than I had in all the twenty-nine years of his life. I learned about his hopes, his dreams, his disappointments. And his loves. His love of country, of medicine and, of course, his family. And one woman who'd always been very special to him."

Here Bram's gaze settled on Dani for a long, unsettling time. Hot tears welled at the backs of her eyelids. She bit her lip but did not look away.

"I hope that, if Ryan were here today, he would tell you he'd discovered a few things about his older brother, as well. But—" Bram drew in a long, ragged breath "—today is not about me. It's about my brother. And I know that there are things he would want me to say to you."

Bram paused. His hands were holding on to either side of the lectern and as Dani watched, his knuckles whitened. She found herself wishing she could see his eyes.

"I believe Ryan would tell you not to mourn him. Because he is not gone. He is living in the hearts of all those who knew him—his family, his friends, the patients whose lives he saved in his beloved emergency room, and the spirits of those he tried to save but could not.

"He would assure you that he will always—for all eternity—be with you. On the brightest sun-filled day and the darkest night. That when the wind sighing in the treetops fans your cheek, it will be his breath, whispering your name. That when the soft summer rain cools your heated temple, it will be his spirit passing by."

Dani heard Bram's deep voice crack. She watched him struggle for control, and win.

"My brother would tell you not to mourn his death." Bram took off his glasses and his dark blue eyes tenderly caressed first his mother, then his stoic father, before turning unreadable again as they settled once more on Dani.

"Instead, he would want you to celebrate life. Because—and I know he believed this with every fiber of his being—someday, we will all meet again." There wasn't a sound to be heard, save for Amanda's soft weeping. Dani pressed her fingers against her mouth to hold back the sob that was struggling to escape her throat.

Then, blessedly, the priest rose to resume the funeral mass, shattering the suspended silence.

In deference to the icy temperature and falling snow, the graveside services were kept brief. The weather also fortuitously grounded the helicopters hired by the army of tabloid reporters. Thanks to Bram's Hollywood fame, what should have been a private family affair had turned into a media event. And then it was over. In an ironic, painful twist of fate, on the very day they'd planned to gather in the Fortune home to celebrate a marriage, the mountain community came together to mourn a death.

As she numbly accepted condolences, Dani realized that Bram, who'd spoken not a word to her since that fateful day, was quietly, methodically getting drunk. Although he remained apart from the others, she was aware of an increasingly dangerous aura surrounding him.

He reminded her of a keg of powder whose fuse had been lit. The question was not *if* Bram Fortune was going to explode, but *when*.

She cornered him alone in the kitchen, where he'd gone to fortify his coffee. The counters were overflowing with food that hadn't fit onto the dining room table.

"You're going to break your mother's heart," she scolded.

"What makes you think I haven't already?" He poured a generous splash of Irish whiskey into the dark brew, took a taste, then added more.

Bram looked, Dani considered, almost as bad as she felt. Which meant he looked absolutely terrible. His face, which she remembered as having always been darkly tanned, even in the dead of winter, was ashen. The lines of a man older than his thirty-five years bracketed his rigid, downturned mouth.

"Goddamn mountain." Bram took another long drink. "I tried to tell him...."

He shook his head and muttered a low, inarticulate string of curses. He was weaving dangerously on his feet.

"You need some fresh air," Dani decided, grateful for something to do to take her mind off the dark cloud of pain.

"In case you haven't noticed, sweetheart," he said, waving his cup toward the gingham-framed windows, "it's snowing." A splash of liquor-spiked coffee sloshed onto the front of his white dress shirt. "Goddamn snow."

In the other room Dani could hear Ryan's mother's soft weeping begin again and knew she couldn't allow Bram to make an already bad situation worse.

"We can go for a drive," she suggested.

He straightened, with obvious effort, and looked down at her. "You and me?"

"Why not? I could use some time away from here myself."

His eyes suddenly cleared, like the sun coming from behind pewter clouds; he was looking down into her face. Looking deep.

They could hear the steady murmur of conversation—Amanda's faint weeping, the voices of friends and family trying impotently to comfort—on the other side of the oak swing door.

"Where's your coat?"

"In the other room."

"Here." Bram grabbed his shearling-lined jacket from a hook beside the door and tossed it over her shoulders. "This'll have to do."

He plucked the whiskey bottle from the counter, then paused long enough to retrieve a six-pack of Miller from the refrigerator before leading her outside into the driving snow.

"Shouldn't we tell everyone that we're leaving?"

"They're all intelligent people. Don't worry, they'll figure it out soon enough."

"What about all those reporters camped out at the bottom of the hill?"

"We'll take the back road. Ryan and I rented the only two four-wheel-drive trucks in town. Even if those ghouls do catch us leaving, their cars will never be able to manage the drifts."

"I don't think going off like this without telling anyone is a very good idea."

"I think it's a dandy idea. Besides, you think anyone in there wants to talk to me? The hometown Hollywood big shot who couldn't save his own brother's life?" His words were slurred with alcohol.

"You're drunk."

"Not yet," he corrected. "But with any luck, I damn well should be soon."

He opened the door of the red Blazer parked in the driveway. "Hop up, sweetheart." He shoved upward on her bottom, pushing her onto the front seat. "Let's get the hell out of here."

He slammed her door shut with more force than necessary, crossed in front of the Blazer, flung open the driver's door and climbed up beside her.

"Where's the damn key?" he muttered, lifting his hips off the seat to thrust his hand deep into the pocket of his slacks. "Okay. Here it is."

He went to jam it into the ignition, hitting the steering column instead. "Dammit." Another try was no more successful.

On the third attempt, Dani reached out and grabbed the key ring from his hand.

"What the hell do you think you're doing?" he growled savagely.

When he grabbed for the keys, Dani held them out of reach. "Your mother's already lost one son. I'm not going to contribute to her losing another. If you want to go for a drive to clear your head, fine. But I'm driving."

"The hell you are!" He lunged for the keys.

She continued to hold them out of reach. The jacket he'd flung over her shoulders slid to the floor.

As Bram glared at her, masculine fury glittering in his suddenly clear eyes, Dani had a very good idea what it would feel like to tease a wild tiger.

He moved toward her, forcing her to retreat until her back was pressed against the passenger door.

"I'm going to ask one more time," he said in a soft, treacherous voice. "And then, if you don't hand over those keys like a good little girl, I won't be responsible for the consequences." He loomed above her, his square jaw set, his eyes the deep, dark blue of the sea at dusk. His thighs, his stomach, his chest, were pressed against hers in a way that was anything but soothing. Outside the truck, a wet, fitful snow blew against the windshield.

The expression on Bram's face might have had any other woman trembling. But not Dani. She'd come a long way since her marriage. She'd vowed never to let any man frighten her again.

Besides, despite his threatening demeanor and his obnoxious attitude, Dani sensed that Bram Fortune would never actually harm a woman. That inner knowledge gave her the edge she needed.

Her chin went up a defiant notch.

"I'm not a girl."

"You know, now that you bring it up, I guess you have grown up some," he agreed. His gaze moved over her with agonizing slowness. "I suppose that's some consolation," he decided. "Knowing that Ryan was getting it regular before he died."

His fingers trailed slowly down the side of her face. Dani jerked away from his touch and slammed the back of her head against the passenger-door window.

A furious sound choked in her throat. "You're disgusting."

"Probably," Bram agreed with a slow sardonic smile she wanted to slap off his mouth. "But then again, life's pretty damn disgusting these days, wouldn't you say?"

Reminding herself that she wanted to keep him away from the house, Dani had no alternative but to put up with his outrageous behavior. For now. But that didn't mean she had to put her own life in jeopardy.

"Dammit, Bram, would you quit being so difficult. After what happened to Ryan, it would kill your mother if you got in an accident because you'd been drinking and driving."

Bram's face hardened. But Dani, who was watching him carefully in the dusky twilight, caught the flicker of acknowledgement—and pain—in his eyes.

"If you let me drive, you can drink all you want," she coaxed.

He didn't immediately respond. Time crawled and still his steady, brooding gaze remained riveted on her face.

"Ryan always said you were a lot smarter than you looked," Bram said finally. "I guess the kid was right."

Dani let out a breath she'd been unaware of holding. "I believe I'll take that as a compliment. Backhanded as it was." She suspected, rightfully so, that he was frugal with them.

"Take it any way you want."

Although it took some intimate maneuvering, they managed to change places.

"Okay, let's get the hell outta here."

He pulled the tab on one of the gold metallic cans of beer. Foam spewed across the back of his hand; Bram licked it off his skin and settled back, his long legs stretched out in front of him.

"I'm not going anywhere until you put on your seat belt."

"Lord, you are a bossy thing." His gaze moved from her stubborn face to her breasts, separated by the wide black belt. "Did you drag my brother around by the balls this way?"

"It wasn't necessary," she countered, refusing to rise to his filthy insinuation. The temperature of her voice dropped a cool thirty degrees, but fire flared in her eyes. "Ryan wasn't some reckless Hollywood hotshot who thought rules and laws and tenets of morality were for the other guy."

Bram tilted the beer back and took a long, thirsty swallow, looking at her over the top of the can. "So my brother's sexy little kitten has claws," he taunted softly. "Interesting."

Dani tossed her head. "Are you fastening that seat belt, or would you rather just sit here in the driveway and insult me?"

Realizing that she truly had no intention of moving from his parents' driveway, he yanked on the seat belt, pulled it across his chest, slammed the metal clasp into the plastic holder and shot her a hot angry glare.

"Satisfied?"

She was, but knowing better than to gloat, Dani put the car into gear. Or tried to.

Accustomed to the automatic shift on her own compact car, she tried to remember back to the long-ago day when Ryan had taught her to shift gears in his father's pickup. Her first attempt was less than successful.

"Jeez," Bram muttered. "I figured you knew how to drive."

"I do."

She tried again, managed it this time, but let the clutch out too fast. The Blazer bounced to a shuddering stop.

"It's a good thing we're not in any hurry," Bram drawled. "Because at this rate, it'll take you the rest of the afternoon to get out of the driveway."

He downed the entire can of beer in long chugs, tossed the can over his shoulder into the back seat and opened another.

Seething, Dani twisted the key again, grinding the engine, but managing to make it through the first three gears without any further delays.

The gravel back road leading down the steep hill from the Fortune house was slick with new-fallen snow but the four-wheel-drive traction hugged the ground, giving Dani confidence.

After stopping at the bottom of the hill, she breathed a sigh of relief when she managed to put the truck into the proper gear on the very first try. Dani supposed that shifting a truck was a lot like riding through the gaits on a horse. After a while, the technique came back to you.

"Where to?" she asked.

"The cabin."

"Your cabin?" She missed second, struggled, and finally settled for third.

"What's the matter?" Bram asked as the truck bumped unhappily along in a gear too high for its prudent speed. "Afraid to be all alone in some remote cabin with me?"

His smooth taunt hit a little too close to home. Dani would have thrown herself into the nearest snowbank before admitting that vague warnings had been whispering up her nerve ends from the moment she'd encountered Bram in the kitchen.

"Of course not," she insisted, not quite truthfully. "It's just that I didn't know you still owned the cabin."

He'd built it himself, she recalled. Back when she and Ryan were still in junior high school. Dani remembered the frustration she'd felt that summer at having lost her best friend. Ryan had hung around the construction site every day, eager to help his big brother. No task had been too unpleasant, no job too dirty.

Furious, Dani had spent the long, lonely vacation sticking pins into a Bram Fortune voodoo doll she'd created from papier mâché, an old high school yearbook photo of her nemesis and some strands of dark hair she'd swiped from his brush.

Her heated curses and muttered incantations had proved steadfastly ineffectual, but eventually Labor Day came and went, Bram returned to college in Los Angeles and Dani had Ryan all to herself again.

Her lips curved in a faint, unconscious smile as she thought how she'd welcomed Ryan back into her charmed circle without so much as making him beg her forgiveness. Well, perhaps, in truth, he had been encouraged to beg. But just a little.

"I never got around to selling it." Bram's deep voice jerked Dani back to the present. "Besides, I like having a place to get away to from time to time. And for the record, whatever might happen in the cabin could happen just as well right here in the truck."

"I realize that."

Bram flashed her a wicked smile. "I remember a time when you two were still in high school and I saw Ryan's truck parked out by the wetlands. From the way the windows were steamed up, I decided that my baby brother must have grown up."

Hot furious color flooded her cheeks. "Ryan and I were in love," she practically spat at him. "And if you continue to degrade what we had together, I'm going to kick you out of this truck and make you walk home."

He was insufferable. Dani wondered, as she had for so many years, exactly what it was Ryan had found to admire in his older brother.

She also wished she still had the voodoo doll.

Muttering something unintelligible that could have been either a curse or grudging acceptance of her terms, Bram yanked off his navy tie, tossed it into the back seat, and unbuttoned the top two buttons of his starched white dress shirt.

Then he settled back and began working his way through the six-pack.

3

THE CABIN WAS ON the bank of a stream in a grove of silver-trunked aspen. The creek was a frozen shimmering ribbon; beside the stream, sword ferns sheathed with frost sparkled silver and blue. In the distance, snow-clouded peaks were etched against the dark winter sky.

The night she and Ryan had graduated from high school, Ryan had borrowed the key from his brother—who, having graduated from UCLA's film school, was off in Mexico, directing his first movie. That coming-of-age story of a young man who'd wanted more from life than working on his father's shrimp boat, had earned Bram his first Oscar.

Telling her mother that she and Ryan would be attending an all-night party at a girlfriend's house, Dani had spent a blissful night in the arms of the only boy she'd ever loved.

Bittersweet memories flooded back, bringing hot tears to her eyes. When a tear trailed down her cheek, Dani surreptitiously brushed it away with her fingers, casting a cautious glance Bram's way, to see if he'd noticed.

But no, he was drinking his damn beer and staring out the passenger window at the snow-draped conifers, lost in some private thoughts of his own.

As she pulled the Blazer up in front of the cabin, a thought occurred to her. "I hope you remembered to bring the key."

"Of course." Another beer can joined the others on the back seat floor. Then he was out of the truck, forging through the drifted snow, leaving her to follow.

Her black suede pumps were not made for hiking in snow and ice. Intent on keeping her feet reasonably dry, Dani tried to stay in Bram's footprints.

But his stride was a great deal longer than hers, and as she approached the door, her high heel landed on ice, rather than packed snow, causing her feet to fly out from under her and she tumbled, bottom first, into a snowbank.

When he heard her startled curse, Bram turned around. His chiseled lips curved into a slow grin that infuriated her.

"And here I thought you were one of the few women who wouldn't stoop to throwing yourself at my feet."

She struggled to push herself out of the snow and managed to get to her feet when she heard her high heel crack, and swearing, she went back down again.

The sides of the drift caved in, covering her with snow. When she tried to kick it off her, her skirt tangled high on her thighs, revealing long slender legs clad in ebony panty hose.

All the time, Bram stood there, whiskey bottle under his arm, looking, for the first time in days, as if he was enjoying himself. "*Tsk, tsk*," he said. "Such language. Didn't your mama ever teach you that well-brought-up ladies don't cuss like loggers?"

The snow was soaking through her dress and her nylons, she'd lost her shoes, and her legs were turning into icicles. "Manners aren't exactly at the top of my list right now," she ground out.

"In that case—" He tossed the bottle into the snow, reached down, took her by the shoulders, jerked her to her feet and hauled her against him.

Dani struck out blindly, but Bram easily grabbed her wrist. Furious, she pushed against his shoulder with her free hand. "If you even dare—"

Her warning was cut off as Bram bent down and took her mouth completely.

His lips were chapped and rough against hers. Long dark fingers ripped out the pins that held her hair in a tidy twist at the nape of her neck. One by one they fell to the ground, sinking into the snow, forgotten.

While his right hand tangled in the long silk strands, bending her head back and arching her body so that her breasts pressed against his hard chest, his left hand was roaming down to her hips, lifting her into the cradle of his thighs, pressing her against the hot, aroused flesh that strained against his slacks.

He forced her lips apart, his teeth grinding against hers. Dani tasted beer and whiskey, anger and frustration. His tongue, not gentle, raked her teeth, the inner lining of her lips, before thrusting deep into her mouth. He was devouring her, his lips drawing out all her intimate secrets.

Despite her fear, despite her fury, somewhere in the far reaches of her mind Dani admitted that Bram Fortune's kiss was doing things to her that no mere kiss had ever done before.

A thick syrupy longing seemed to have replaced her blood; the hot, insistent flow of desire running through her veins left her too weak to keep up her struggle.

Dani's body sagged against his; her hands, squeezed into tight fists to push him away, opened and her fingers curled, gathering up bunches of crisp white dress shirt before clawing their way up to his shoulder, into his hair.

When the kiss grew deeper, then deeper still, Dani moaned in panicked excitement. Bram's hunger, and the rawness of that hunger, thrilled her. Terrified her. Needs ripped through her body.

Her pain, which she'd kept bottled up for days, flowed out of her and into him. His anger flared out of him and into her.

Somewhere in a nearby treetop a blue jay scolded furiously; immersed in these shattering sensations, Dani barely heard it.

Although she would later find it hard to believe, all coherent thought had fled her mind. She forgot who she was,
who he was. There was only this frightening, thrilling, in-
trinsically dangerous pleasure.

Gradually, as if he'd sensed her surrender, the force went
out of the kiss, but not the power. Dani clung to him, accepting this forbidden ecstasy, accepting him. And then she
was freed so quickly, she staggered and had to grab his arm
to keep from falling back into the snow.

"I don't understand."

Her hand trembled as she dragged it through her tangled
hair and looked up at him. Falling snow sparkled in his thick
hair, his mouth was back in its grim line, all the heated emotion had disappeared from his eyes.

"That sure as hell makes two of us," he said. "Because believe me, sweetheart, you are definitely not my type."

She tossed her head, causing two more pins to disappear
into the drifted snow. "You're not my type, either."

"So you've said. Then there shouldn't be any problem,
should there?"

"Not at all," Dani agreed stiffly.

"Fine."

His alert eyes observed her slight shiver. "You're soaked
through to the skin. We'd better get you inside and in front
of a fire before you get pneumonia."

The uncharacteristic regard for her comfort and health
surprised Dani. "Thank you. That's very thoughtful of you."

"I'm never thoughtful." He retrieved the key to the cabin
from his pocket and opened the door. "It's just that I don't
think I could handle two funerals in one week."

They entered the darkened cabin that seemed even colder
than the outdoors. Bram flicked a switch beside the door and
appeared unsurprised when the lights failed to go on. "The
power goes out a lot up here in the winter," he informed her,

as he lit a lantern hanging by the door. "The snow knocks down the lines."

He picked up the receiver of the telephone on a nearby table, listened, then returned it to the cradle. "Phone's out, too."

Terrific, Dani considered. Now no one would know where they were.

"I'll start a fire."

"Th-thank y-you." Her teeth were chattering and now that the last remnant of heat from their kiss had disintegrated, she felt chilled to the bone.

Bram looked up from where he was squatting before the stone fireplace and gave her a sweeping, yet strangely remote look. "I'd offer you a hot bath, but the water would be cold. But you probably should get out of that wet dress."

Her hands clutched at the front of the wet wool. "I would have thought a man with your outrageous reputation with women could think of a better line than that."

"For chrissakes, Dani," Bram said on a burst of frustrated air. "From the time I discovered the reason for the differences between boys and girls, I've never had to force or trick a woman into my bed.

"And if you actually believe that I'd begin with my dead brother's fiancée, you're even crazier than I've always thought you were."

He turned back to the task at hand. "There's a battery-operated lantern in the bathroom," he informed her brusquely. "And a robe. Put it on and we can hang your dress in front of the fire to dry."

Not at all willing to slip into some filmy negligee one of his lovers had left behind, Dani was relieved to see that the robe hanging on a hook on the back of the plank door was a man's white terry-cloth one.

Although the hem nearly reached the floor, and the sleeves fell below the tips of her fingers, the robe was a decided im-

provement over her wet dress. Bram had worn it recently,
Dani determined. The thick material smelled of the same
pine-scented soap she'd noticed clinging to his skin when he'd
kissed her.

When she unconsciously lifted the wide lapel and buried
her face into the fabric, she experienced a renewed flare of
desire that left her shaken.

As she began peeling off her sodden panty hose, Dani
struggled to put these unsettling feelings in their proper per-
spective.

Ryan's death had left a giant hole inside her. And Bram,
being Bram, couldn't resist an opportunity to seduce a
woman. Any woman.

The kiss hadn't had anything to do with her, Dani decided. A rake at heart, he'd merely responded in character
when he'd seen her sprawled in that snowdrift, her skirt high
on her thighs.

She'd never liked him. And she certainly hadn't wanted
him to kiss her.

So why had she kissed him back? Dani stopped undressing.

There was a knock on the door. "You all right?" Bram's
gruff voice called in to her.

"I'm fine."

"You sure? You've been in there an awfully long time."

"Taking off wet panty hose isn't easy."

"Want some help?"

"No, thank you."

"Suit yourself. But if you plan to stay in there much longer,
let me know, okay? Because I've drunk a lot of beer that's
beginning to back up on me."

"So go outside and write your name in the snow."

She dragged the sodden panty hose the rest of the way
down her legs and yanked them off her feet. Her diamond

engagement ring caught in the nylon, ripping a long ladder up the left calf.

She tossed the ruined panty hose into the wastebasket. Then, unwilling to take orders, Dani stayed where she was, counting slowly to one hundred in English, then in French.

When she finally exited the bathroom, she found the cabin empty. Obviously, Bram had taken her up on her suggestion.

Dani draped her dress over the back of a chair and pulled it near the fire Bram had started in the massive stone fireplace. The flames crackled invitingly, the scent of cedar filled the room.

Dani held her hands, palms out, toward the fire, enjoying the soothing warmth. A fur rug was spread in front of the hearth; she remembered that sometime during that long-ago graduation night, Ryan had told her that the rogue black bear had been shot by his great-grandfather after attacking two lumberjacks working in a remote logging camp.

Sinking down onto the rug, Dani began to cry silently. Tears streamed down her cheeks; her slender shoulders, engulfed in oversize folds of terry cloth, shook.

She heard the door open behind her, felt a gust of icy wind and realized that Bram was back. Unwilling to let him see her this way, and still irritated by the way he had taken advantage of her vulnerable emotional state, she rubbed at her wet face with the backs of her hands and refused to turn around.

"That storm's getting worse," he informed her. "I thought I'd better bring in some more wood, since it looks as if we're going to have to spend the night."

Forgetting that she hadn't intended to pay the least bit of attention to him, Dani shot him a startled glance. During the time she'd been in the bathroom, he'd changed into a pair of worn jeans and a black L.A. Raiders sweatshirt. On his feet, instead of the black dress shoes he'd worn to his brother's funeral, were a pair of scuffed cowboy boots.

"There is no way that I'm spending the night with you," Dani insisted hotly. "I'd rather sleep with Bigfoot!"

"You're not exactly my stranded-in-a-remote-cabin fantasy woman, either, baby," he retorted. "But from the way that white stuff is piling up out there, it doesn't look as if we have much choice." He dumped the split logs onto the floor beside the fireplace. "So we're stuck with one another. Whether we like it or not." Kneeling, he began arranging the fragrant logs into a neat pile.

"After what happened to Ryan, everyone will be frantic if we don't come back," Dani warned.

"I already took care of that."

"How?"

"I called the house on the cellular phone I had in the Blazer, told Dad where we were, and that we were safe, and that we'd try to make it out of here in the morning."

"I didn't know you had a cellular phone."

"Now you do."

"You could have asked him to ask John Carpenter to get out his snowplow and clear the road."

"I could have," he agreed. "But nearly everyone in town is wrung out, both physically and emotionally, from Ryan's death. I figured, rather than dragging some helpful soul out into another damn snowstorm, you and I could call a temporary truce."

He had, she hated to admit, a point. "I didn't realize you ever thought of anyone else."

"I have my moments."

Dani watched him continue to stack the logs and almost against her will she remembered how those strong dark hands had felt against her hips, holding her against him, creating a slow-burning, tantalizing heat.

"You didn't have to stop crying on my account," he said.

"I wasn't crying."

He shot her a quick glance. "Then how come it looks as if you're wearing red eyeliner? And your nose looks like Rudolph's?"

"With compliments like that, I'm amazed you manage to lure so many women into your bed."

"I hadn't realized you were looking for compliments," he countered. "I seem to recall a woman who looked an awfully lot like you saying she'd rather sleep with Bigfoot." He smiled mirthlessly. "Perhaps that was your evil twin."

He positioned the last log on the stack, rocked back on his heels and admired his handiwork.

"Now that that little chore is taken care of," he said, turning to Dani, "maybe I can try out a few of those pretty phrases you seem to be asking for."

She jerked back when he ran his hand down her hair. "I'm not asking for anything from you," she insisted. "Are you always this insufferable?"

"Only when I lose my only brother," he countered.

A silence dropped between them like a thick curtain. Cursing under his breath, Bram stood and went over to a counter and picked up the whiskey bottle he'd retrieved from the snowbank.

"You know, that really isn't going to help," Dani offered.

"You ever been drunk?"

"Of course not."

"Then what the hell makes you an expert?" He unscrewed the black top, tilted the bottle back and swallowed. When he lowered the bottle, a defiant gleam shone in his eyes. "I'll make you a deal."

"What?"

"You grieve for Ryan your way, and I'll grieve in mine. And tomorrow we'll see which one of us feels like trying to keep on living."

The depth of his pain, evident in his voice and on his face, surprised her. "I didn't realize you cared that much."

He shook his head, then took another drink. "She didn't know I cared. Hell, the kid was my brother. How could I not care? I loved him, dammit!"

Without warning, he flung the bottle in her direction. Before she could duck, it went flying by her head.

The glass shattered against the stone, the whiskey spattered onto the flames, sending them shooting upward in an orange-and-red alcoholic flare.

"Nice special effects," Dani said slowly, the shock still reverberating through her.

She realized the gesture had not been meant to hurt, or even shock. It had been a spontaneous emotional release, pure and simple. She wished she could do something to lessen the tumultuous feelings bottled up inside her.

"No wonder you're such a famous, hotshot director."

He stared at her for a full thirty seconds. And then tossed back his head and laughed loud and long up at the beamed ceiling.

When he looked down at her again, his eyes were wet with tears. Tears of laughter or pain, Dani couldn't tell. He picked up the pack of cigarettes from the table and held it out toward her. When she refused with a shake of her head, he shook one out and lit it.

"Last fall," Bram said, crossing the room to sit beside her on the rug, "after you and my brother made your engagement official, Ryan came down to L.A. to ask me to be his best man.

"We went out to dinner and over a ridiculously expensive goat-cheese pizza, I asked him why in the world a sensible, upstanding doctor such as himself was marrying some flighty divorced artist. Even if she did have world-class legs."

Dani had two choices. She could challenge him on his unflattering description or she could remain silent and avoid ruining the first reasonably peaceful moment they'd shared all day. She chose the latter.

"What did he say?"

"He said there were more reasons than he could count." Bram was staring thoughtfully into the flames. He blew out a plume of smoke. "But he supposed that if he were forced to come up with one overriding reason that he'd fallen in love with you, it was that you made him laugh."

He turned to her, his expression grave. "He told me that there was something wonderful about lying together after making love and laughing. At everything and nothing."

The tears she hadn't wanted to reveal to Bram returned, hot and insistent. "Thank you," she managed past the painful lump in her throat, "for telling me that. I never knew."

Bram reached out and with a tenderness she never would have suspected he possessed, brushed a tear off her cheek with the pad of his thumb. "He never told you?"

"No." Unnerved by what should have been an unthreatening touch, along with the sympathy she saw in his gaze, Dani turned and stared at the dancing red-and-orange flames. "He didn't."

"I suppose he figured he had lots of time to tell you how he felt."

Unable to answer, Dani pressed her lips together and nodded.

Bram ground out the cigarette, lay on his back beside her and flung his arm over his eyes. "You know, sometimes life really sucks."

Dani silently concurred.

They remained that way—Dani staring into the hypnotic flickering flames, Bram with his eyes covered—both lost in their own painful thoughts.

"Did he ever tell you about the first time Dad let him go deer hunting with us?" Bram asked after a time.

Dani sighed—a soft, painful little sigh. "No."

"He was fourteen," Bram said. "All freckles and braces and cowlicks. He'd spent the entire summer shooting up so fast, the rest of his body hadn't grown with him. He looked like a lodgepole pine."

"I remember the braces," Dani said quietly. "I had them, too. One Fourth of July at Commons Beach, we were kissing during the fireworks and got them caught. I was terrified that we were going to have to call the fire department to separate us."

"It would've taken a lot more than the fire department to ever separate you two," Bram decided. "Mom always called you and Ryan Siamese twins. I think she knew before you two did that you'd get married someday."

He'd said the words off the top of his head, without thinking, and immediately regretted them. He opened his eyes and turned his head toward her. "I'm sorry."

"I know what you meant." Dani drew her legs up against her chest and wrapped her arms around them. Resting her cheek on her knees, she looked over at him. "Tell me about the hunting trip."

"There was a group of us. Dad, Ryan, my cousin Johnny, Danny Ames and his dad, and me. We were all going to split up, but since it was Ryan's first trip, Dad told me to take him along with me. To show him the ropes."

A log fell in the grate, creating a shower of sparks. Bram pushed himself to his feet, picked up the poker and lifted it back into place.

"It was getting toward the end of the day. Ryan, still as excited as a kid on Christmas Eve to be out with the guys, was out in front of me. We were headed back to the truck and I wasn't in a very good mood. It had definitely been a less-than-successful day. We must have tramped for miles without seeing so much as a fawn or a doe.

"And then I looked up and saw Ryan, standing like a stone statue, his gun pointed toward the underbrush. He reminded me of a bird dog at point."

Satisfied that the log would remain where he'd shoved it, Bram sat down beside Dani again. "I looked in the direction of his gun barrel, and there, no more than fifty yards away, was the biggest buck I ever saw. With a rack at least this wide." He put his palms up, three feet apart.

"I don't remember Ryan ever shooting a deer."

"That's because he didn't. I waited for him to pull the trigger, knowing he'd never have a better opportunity drop into his lap if he lived to be a hundred.

"That's when I realized that there was no way in hell that my baby brother was going to be able to shoot that deer."

"So I suppose you did?"

He gave her a pained look. "No, actually I didn't. To tell the truth, I was kind of enjoying just looking at that magnificent buck myself. But then I heard the others headed our way and I knew it was only a matter of seconds before one of them would catch sight of him."

"What happened?"

"I fired over the buck's head and he took off."

"You did that? For an animal?"

"A magnificent animal," Bram explained. "I figured I'd solved the problem neatly enough, but then I noticed that Ryan didn't say a single word, all the way home. When I asked him about it later, he told me that he was embarrassed about letting me down." Bram shook his head in mute frustration.

"He was always trying to live up to your expectations," Dani agreed softly.

"They were *his* damn expectations," Bram corrected brusquely. "Not mine. Hell, I never wanted Ryan to be like me. In fact there were times, like during that suspended moment on that hunting trip, that I wished I could be more like him."

That thought was so amazing that Dani couldn't come up with an appropriate response.

"Of course, nature being what it is, Ryan couldn't become me, any more than I could become him. But you know something?"

"What?"

"I never went deer hunting again."

Her lips curved into a reluctant smile. Her first in days. "You really did love him, didn't you?"

"Of course, I did. Hell, don't you think I knew that Ryan looked up to me? Why can't you give me credit for realizing the responsibility I had not to fail him?

"I spent years mending my baby brother's broken kites, untangling his fishing lines, all those things that big brothers are always bitching about but secretly love to do.

"But the one time he really needed my help—" Bram dragged his hand wearily over his tortured face, muffling his words "—I couldn't do a damn thing."

When he took his hand away, moisture glistened suspiciously in his eyes. All the animosity Dani had ever felt toward this man vanished, like late-season snow under a hot June sun.

"No one could have predicted that avalanche." She placed her hand on the sleeve of his black sweatshirt, feeling the muscle of his arm tense beneath her fingers. "And no one could have saved him."

Bram looked down at her hand, as if trying to remember to whom it belonged and how it had gotten there. In the flickering light of the fire, the diamond on her fourth finger sparkled like ice. "I remember when Ryan bought this," Bram murmured, toying with the ring. "In Chicago."

"Chicago?" His fingers brushing against hers were inordinately distracting. "I don't remember Ryan ever going to Chicago."

"You were studying in Paris. He was in his second year of medical school and decided you two had been apart enough.

He was planning to surprise you with it when you got back to the States."

"Oh." Her heart plummeted. "I didn't know."

"Ryan figured that out for himself when you wrote him from Monaco and told him you'd gotten married. To someone else."

"I didn't know," she repeated weakly.

She wondered if it would have made a difference. Peter had been so dashing. So seemingly cosmopolitan. He'd also come into her life at a time when she'd been open for adventure. While Ryan represented the familiar. The comfortable. The safe.

She wondered why Ryan had never told her about the ring and decided that he'd wanted to spare her feelings. Or perhaps, she admitted reluctantly, he'd been too hurt by her sudden marriage to another man to discuss it.

"I was filming *Tarnished Vows* in Chicago when Ryan showed up out of the blue wanting my advice on engagement rings just as we were about to film a very pivotal and expensive car-chase scene. Hell, I couldn't take off and go shopping for diamonds."

"I suppose that's what you told him."

"Sure. And right after I set my baby brother straight about schedules and film costs and budgetary responsibility, we went out for coffee and doughnuts while we waited for the jewelry store to open."

Somehow, she wasn't as surprised as she might once have been. "And then what happened?"

"Ryan's girl ultimately got a dynamite ring, picked out by yours truly, by the way, when he couldn't make up his mind between that solitaire and an emerald cut, and the film went two hundred thousand dollars over budget because I was forced to keep an entire crew waiting while it rained buckets for the next three days."

She looked down at her engagement ring. "You picked this out?"

"I told you, Ryan couldn't decide. Finally I got the idea to flip a coin and the solitaire won."

"Oh." She felt strangely relieved. "Then it wasn't a personal decision on your part."

"Of course not. Ryan was the one supposedly getting engaged, not me."

Ryan.

Bram's stroking hand moved from her finger, across the back of her hand, leaving an alien, unsettling trail of heat. Their gazes met and held.

And Dani felt a strange little jolt in her heart.

Inside, the fire crackled; outside the wind moaned. Inside, a storm of another kind was building.

As she struggled to untangle her feelings, Bram's hand slipped beneath the turned-up sleeve of the robe and continued purposefully up her arm.

In the ebony gleam of his pupils, Dani could see the flickering orange flames. And she could also see a tiny miniature of herself, sitting deathly still, caught in his gaze like that long-ago buck.

His hand cupped her shoulder, his fingers massaging her with a practiced touch that both soothed and excited. Dani knew that if she didn't move, right this minute, she would have only herself to blame.

"We can't do this," she insisted shakily. It was only a whisper, but easily heard in the stillness of the cabin.

"You know that." His tantalizing hand brushed up the side of her neck. "And I know that." He observed her solemnly, sadly. "So, do you want to tell me why the idea feels so eminently right?"

There were reasons. Dani knew there had to be reasons. But heaven help her, with his eyes looking so deeply into hers, as if he could see all the way to her soul, she couldn't think of a single one.

"Bram—"

"I like the way you say my name." His thumb brushed against her lips, his touch as light as goose down. "Say it again."

"I can't." She pulled her hand away and was appalled to realize she was trembling. "I loved Ryan. More than anything."

"I loved him, too. As much, in my own way, as you."

The treacherous hand was back again, on her hair, trailing down the side of her neck, following the line of her jaw, leaving heat wherever it roamed.

"But he's gone. And he isn't coming back. And if you ever tell another living soul I told you this, I'll call you a damn liar, but I feel like he's taken the better part of me with him and the part that's left feels like going up on that mountain and staying there until I freeze to death and end up with my brother, wherever he is."

The pain etched into his handsome face was too raw, too ugly to be feigned. Dani put her palm against his cheek.

"I've felt the same way," she admitted. "In fact, I was feeling so horrible and lost and lonely this afternoon that I couldn't stand to be around people anymore.

"I came into that kitchen to escape and if I hadn't found you there and been forced to get you away, I honestly don't know what I might have done."

He laughed at that—a rough, deep, humorless sound that shimmied its way beneath the heavy hem of the robe, up her legs, between her thighs.

"We're a helluva pair, aren't we?" he asked. "Me the Hollywood hotshot and you the up-and-coming toast-of-the-West-Coast art world.

"Anyone looking at us would think we had the world in our eager hands, but the miserable truth is that between the two of us, we can't figure out how the hell we're going to make it through the next twenty-four hours."

He turned his head and pressed his lips against her hand.

"I need you, Dani," Bram said gruffly. "And I think you need me, too. Just for tonight. Just long enough to make the pain go away. For a little while."

Their faces were so close that all it would take was for one of them to move just the slightest bit. For a long, heartfelt moment, they paused on the steep, slippery precipice of temptation.

Then, with a sound somewhere between a curse and a plea, Bram pulled her into his arms and kissed her with a hot, furious passion until, on a ragged sob, Dani flung her arms around his neck, clinging tight as she allowed him—begged him—to take them both over the edge.

4

IT WAS ALL HELL SMOKE and flame and thunder. Her body felt like a furnace.

Somewhere in the back of her mind, Dani knew that there would be a price, a payment of pain, for succumbing to such dark temptation. But as the flames licked at her blood, she knew she had no choice but to submit to this, whatever the cost.

His hands were in her hair, bringing her mouth back to his, again and again, until she was breathless.

Words, low and harsh, poured from him, against her lips, her throat, the silky skin between the lapels of the robe.

Roughly, he tore at the robe, whipping it away, exposing her to his burning gaze. Then his mouth closed around the taut peak of her breast, hot and greedy, creating a shaft of exquisite pain so sharp she cried out, even as she wanted more.

But he'd already moved on, bringing her to desperation with his hands, his lips. He was relentless, nipping and licking and sucking, as if he wanted to leave no part of her untouched, unclaimed.

His mouth moved over her rib cage, across her stomach, lingering just long enough to explore her navel with his wet, hot tongue. His fingers tangled in the downy delta at the top of her thighs while he blew softly, ruffling the ebony hair, cooling and heating her flesh at the same time.

Every inch of the way, Dani knew she should stop him, knew that what they were doing was not only wrong, but unreasonably foolhardy; but the need for comfort warred with reason, and the temptation to explore this incredible feeling further won out over common sense.

As if reading her mind, Bram lifted his head, his eyes meeting hers for a thrilling, suspended moment. The firelight illuminated his face, casting the slash of his cheekbones into shadow. His eyes, so like his brother's, but darker, gleamed cobalt in the flickering glow.

Ryan had always insisted that Dani was the most beautiful woman in the world. Living in a world where each woman on the street seemed more stunning than the last, Bram had never given Danielle Cantrell's appearance any real thought.

But now, as he gazed down at her, he realized Ryan had been right. At this frozen moment in time, Dani was almost more beautiful than a man could bear.

Her hair tumbled freely over her naked shoulders in a torrent of ebony silk. Firelight flickered warmly over flesh the color of alabaster.

If he'd been directing her in a film, he would have created a scene where dark-eyed Gypsies twirled around smoky campfires to the sound of tambourines.

Bram smiled a rogue's smile. Then he kissed her again, a brief, tantalizing, heartbreakingly gentle touching of lips so different from the others they'd shared thus far.

Before she could think about the meaning of that soft, oddly tender kiss, his mouth had continued its sensual quest, creating sparks wherever it roamed. When he nibbled on the smooth flesh at the inside of her thigh, Dani drew in a deep, shuddering breath and bent her leg, offering more.

And then, without warning, he plunged his tongue into her.

Dani stiffened and would have backed away, but Bram slid his hands beneath her hips, digging his fingers into the moist, pliant flesh, holding her, trapping her. His clever, wicked tongue was quick and greedy and she moaned as she arched against his mouth, willing, wanting.

There was nothing soft, nothing gentle about Bram, but Dani didn't want gentleness. What she wanted, what she needed, was this raw primitive power that was like nothing she'd ever felt, or even imagined. For this one night she would suffer no embarrassment, feel no shame.

Coherent thought disintegrated, consumed by the fire storm that had taken over Dani's mind. Her body was heavy with desire; her head light. His fingers slid inside the giving folds of her body, seeking warm intimate secrets while his teeth toyed with the ultrasensitive kernel of flesh, creating a need so sharp she thought she'd surely shatter. Her fingers curled mindlessly at her sides, grabbing handfuls of fur; her thighs trembled, her movements beneath his mouth were abandoned and desperate.

The painful pleasure built, spiraling outward to her fingertips, like shafts of dazzling, blinding light. Her belly grew taut, her thighs tensed, a flush spread over her breasts. It seemed as if every nerve ending in her body was concentrated on that one vital, quivering spot.

A final flick of his tongue against the hard nub caused Dani to be jolted by a violent, shuddering climax.

His jeans and cotton briefs were gone with more speed than was reasonable, but Bram gave her no time to explore his body as he had hers.

His flesh was furnace hot as he took possession of her, his strong, greedy thrusts driving her deeper and deeper into the smoke-filled netherworld.

It was as if he was trying to expunge his grief in her body. Wrapped close, mouths fused, they moved together while the fire rose higher and hotter and then they were swept up together into the inferno. When control fled, Bram shouted her name and Dani sobbed his, in both ecstasy and despair.

The fire had died down; a chill had come over the room. They were still tangled together, damp flesh to damp flesh.

Dani risked a glance upward into Bram's shuttered face and realized that he was already taking back what he'd given her, returning what she'd given him. She wanted to ask him not to shut her out, not yet. She wanted to beg for just a little more time, a brief respite, before she would be forced to confront all that she had lost up there on that mountain.

But she didn't know the words, and doubted that she'd have the nerve to say them, even if she did.

Bram's curse was low and pungent. He closed his eyes for a brief, painful moment, then pulled away from her and began gathering up his clothes. "I owe you an apology."

His brusque tone struck a nerve. "You don't owe me anything." She ran her palm over the fur. The impact of where she was, what they'd done, came crashing down on her. "Oh, God."

"What's wrong?" He'd located his briefs and pulled them up his legs.

What wasn't wrong? The man she loved was dead, barely in his grave, and she'd just betrayed him with his own brother.

Dani took a deep breath, and with a great deal of effort, managed to keep her eyes level and her voice calm. "Nothing that wasn't already wrong."

He yanked on the jeans, zipping them, leaving the top snap unbuttoned. "I knew you'd have regrets."

"I don't have any regrets." Her voice turned cold and remote as she wrapped her arms stiffly around herself in an unconscious gesture of self-protection.

Bram lifted a brow. "It's a bit late to begin throwing up walls now, sweetheart. Since the foundation's already crumbled." He glanced suggestively at the glossy rug. Uncomfortably conscious of her unclad state, Dani began searching for the discarded robe.

"Here." Bram retrieved it from the leather sofa nearly ten feet away, making Dani wonder how on earth it had gotten there. "You're feeling guilty, aren't you?"

"No." She shoved her hands through the sleeves, never minding that the robe was inside out, and tied the sash. "Maybe." Her voice—almost a wail—climbed an octave, trembling every note of the way. "Dammit, of course I am."

Feelings, too many of them to manage, clogged in her throat. When the tears started again, she turned away.

Dani heard his weary sigh, felt the firm, steady touch of his hands on her shoulders.

"It's an automatic thing with you, isn't it?" he murmured.

"What?"

"Guilt. It's a knee-jerk reaction. You feel guilty that you didn't die up on that mountain with my brother, you feel guilty that you tried, in what seemed like a good idea at the time, to expunge some of your guilt and grief by making love with me. Hell, you're probably already feeling guilty for things you haven't even done yet."

He pressed his lips against her hair. "You do the guilt thing really well, Dani. Are you sure you're not Catholic?"

She could hear the smile in his voice, coaxing another one from her.

"Don't you take anything seriously?" The minute she heard the accusation pass her lips, Dani wished she could take it back. "I'm sorry. I keep saying these terrible things to you and I know I shouldn't, because you're hurting, too. But I can't seem to help myself."

He turned her around in his arms and looked down at her, his expression both grave and teasing at the same time. "And now you're going to feel guilty about that, too, aren't you?"

For some reason she couldn't understand, Dani found that she could handle Bram's arrogant chauvinism. It was moments like this, when he was actually trying to be kind, that made her nervous.

"I don't know. Probably," she admitted.

"Poor, confused, hurting Dani." His low, deep voice, edged with roughness, did something warm and wonderful to her name. "We've complicated things, haven't we?"

When he touched a hand to her face, the air in the room seemed to go suddenly still.

A last dying ember flared into a shower of sparks; Dani imagined that she could feel those sparks on her cheek. When his dark fingers trailed down her throat, creating a jump in her pulse, Dani knew that she had to tread carefully.

"I don't see why." She backed away, eyeing Bram as warily as he was eyeing her. "It was only sex, Bram. And although given the same circumstances, I certainly wouldn't do it again, I'm not going to beat myself up about it."

When he gave her a look that lasted far longer than she was comfortable with, Dani realized she was holding her breath.

"Good," was all he said. He turned away, stacked another log on the fire and, squatting down, blew on the embers until a single flame sparked and caught on the dry cedar bark. Dani's eyes were drawn to the muscular thighs molding the soft denim and remembered, all too clearly for her own good, exactly how those legs had felt against hers.

"There's something else," he said when he turned back to her again. He retrieved the pack of cigarettes he kept on the pine mantel, shook one loose and lit it with a kitchen match he struck against the stone fireplace.

"What?"

"It's something I probably should have asked right off the bat, but since you and Ryan were about to get married, I assumed you're on the Pill."

It crossed Dani's mind that he damn well should have asked this question earlier. "Like all your other women?"

Restrained irritation had him practically biting the cigarette in half. "I asked a simple question, Dani. Do you think you could just give me a simple answer?"

She welcomed the anger; it overrode the still-sharp pain of Ryan's death.

"Yes, you should have asked right off the bat," she agreed, managing to control her voice to a cold hard steadiness. "And yes, I'm on the Pill and no, you don't have to worry, because I don't have any sexually transmitted diseases and I'm not going to get pregnant. So you can leave here and go back to Hollywood without so much as a backward glance."

"Now that you bring it up, I don't have anything contagious, either," he added as an afterthought.

"I'm so pleased for you." Sarcasm dripped from her voice. "And surprised, given what I read about your hedonistic lifestyle."

He drew in on the cigarette, his eyes hard as he looked at her through the smoke that rose from it. "You should know better than to believe anything you read in those rags."

A flush of embarrassment rose in her cheeks. "Point taken." She nodded stiffly. "And now that we've exchanged pertinent medical information, why don't we just forget this ever happened, all right?"

Bram gave her another long look. Refusing to be intimidated, Dani stared unflinchingly back at him.

"If that's what you really want, fine, we'll forget it." He flicked the cigarette into the fireplace, then crossed the room to the compact open kitchen. "How about some supper? I've got a propane camp stove I use as a backup when the power's out. I can heat up a can of soup and make sandwiches."

"I'm not hungry."

"You should have something. You've hardly eaten anything in days."

"I didn't realize you'd noticed."

"Oh, I've noticed a great deal about you, Dani."

As he gave her another slow, seductive look, another burst of anger flared. How easily he tapped into her temper! She and Ryan had never so much as argued; so how was it that his brother could bring her to the boiling point with only a word or a look?

Dani closed her eyes, willing her system to calm. "Did you mention supper?"

Somehow, they managed to get through the rest of the evening without any more flare-ups.

Over a surprisingly tasty canned clam chowder and thick roast beef on a nutty whole wheat bread, she told him about the gallery owner who'd professed enthusiastic belief in her work.

When Bram asked about her time in Paris, she briefly touched on her student days. She did not mention Peter.

While they waited for water to boil for instant coffee, he told her about the movie he was currently making. He did not mention the letter-writing campaign.

"Sounds like nice family fare," she murmured. Unwillingly, she thought of Peter. Her blood went cold.

Not knowing the details of her marriage, Bram merely shrugged. "Not all marriages are as happy as my folks'."

Dani, who had firsthand confirmation of that gritty fact, didn't respond.

After a slight argument over sleeping arrangements, it was agreed that Dani would sleep on the pullout sofa bed in front of the fire while Bram would take the nearby chair.

Overcome with exhaustion and emotion, Dani fell immediately to sleep.

The dream came before dawn. She was in San Francisco. In the bedroom of the Pacific Heights palazzo that had been built by some long-ago Bannister ancestor after the 1906 earthquake. Through the Palladian windows she could see the dark forests of the Presidio, and beyond, one of the world's most coveted vistas: the soaring orange span of the Golden Gate Bridge, the cerulean bay and the iridescent, fog-silvered hills beyond.

A man stood beside the window, his handsome face twisted with rage.

They'd been to an afternoon wine-tasting to raise funds for the symphony. It had been the first time she'd been out in public for weeks and Dani had made the mistake of enjoying herself.

"I saw you," Peter said softly. Dangerously.

Dread was an iron fist, squeezing painfully at her heart. "Saw me?" Neither her innocent confusion, nor her fear, were feigned.

"I saw you flirting with Richard Crocker."

Dani breathed a sigh of relief. Was that all? *You can handle this,* she assured herself.

"His wife bought one of my paintings last year. An oil of the little girl at the cherry festival in Japantown. You remember the one."

"I remember. I thought it was clichéd."

The words stung. She had to force the conciliatory smile. "I guess the Crockers have taste that leans toward the clichéd." Personally, she had thought the colorful scene one of her best works. "Anyway, Richard was telling me how much they enjoy it."

"Sure." His tone was thick with disbelief.

A frisson of fear began to shimmer its all-too-familiar way up her spine. "It's the truth."

"Liar." The vicious slap stung across her cheekbone. "You were practically inviting the bastard to go to bed with you." Another slap. This one a backhanded blow that had her head reeling.

"No!"

"Don't lie to me." His fingers curled around her chin, holding her fearful gaze to his. "You were seducing him, right there in front of God and everyone. And he was undressing you with his eyes, looking at you like he knew exactly what was under that demure little dress you wore to throw me off track."

She ran her now sweaty hands down the front of the long-sleeved, high-necked, calf-length black linen dress so unlike the bright-colored clothing she'd favored before her marriage. If the garment were any more demure, it would have qualified as an Iranian *chador*.

"You bought me this dress. At Saks. Just last week." She gave him a coaxing smile. "Remember?"

"I remember buying it. But not so other men can take it off you." His hand curled around her throat.

She shook her head. "There have never been any other men, Peter. Not since the day I met you."

"Why the hell should I believe a tramp like you?" His fingers tightened. Tomorrow there would be bruises. There always were. "You weren't a virgin when I met you." Dani had long rued the day she'd made the mistake of telling Peter—at his insistence—about the only other man in her life.

"I saw you laughing with him. About me."

She'd had this conversation too many times to count. "Not about you," she insisted. "Never about you." Another truth. Absolutely nothing about her marriage to Peter Bannister was a laughing matter.

He backed up and gave her a long, considering look. "You've been a very bad girl, Dani."

She opened her mouth to protest, saw the murder in his eyes and immediately shut it again.

"A very bad girl." He began unfastening his gold-and-diamond cuff links. Dani watched as he rolled up his sleeves.

"Peter, please—"

"You'll have to be punished."

When he slipped his alligator belt slowly, threateningly from the loops of his linen slacks, she turned to run.

But he was quicker, catching her flowing hair from behind before she could reach the door.

The unattractive dress was ripped from her back. The thin black belt slashed across her bare flesh. His fists followed. And he was hitting. And hitting. And hitting.

It was her screams that woke him. Bram jumped up, disoriented. Then it all came crashing down on him.

He was in the cabin.

With his brother's fiancée. Whom he'd seduced.

And who was currently screaming bloody murder.

Intent on soothing her night fears, he tried to gather her into his arms. But she was hitting out at him, her fists flailing, her eyes wide with terror.

"Dammit, Dani!" He caught both her hands and braceleted them with one of his. With his free hand he began stroking the tangled ebony cloud of her hair. "It's only a dream. A nightmare."

But she wouldn't stop fighting. With her hands imprisoned, she began kicking out at him.

It was almost as if she were fighting for her life. Bram had no way of knowing that in Dani's mind, she was doing precisely that.

"Dammit!" When one heel caught him in the groin, he gave up trying to be gentle and flung his body atop hers, pinning her to the mattress.

"It's a dream," he repeated over and over. "Only a bad dream."

His words gradually made their way through the cold mists fogging her mind. Dani became aware of the hard, strangely familiar body pressed against hers. She felt his fingers stroking her face, across the ridge of cheekbone that had been reconstructed after Peter's fists had shattered it.

"Look," he said, "I'm going to let go of your hands." He did as promised. "There. Better?"

"I think so." She pressed her own palm against the side of his face. His unshaven face felt like sandpaper to her touch. Comprehension slowly sank in. "Bram?"

"Bingo." His rewarding smile was a flash of white in the predawn darkness. "Got it on the first try."

For not the first time, Dani found him much more disconcerting when he was being kind. "I'm sorry."

She felt warm and soft and discomfitingly appealing beneath him. Bram could have stayed like this the rest of the night.

"Don't give it a second thought." He reluctantly sat up. "Like I said, it was just a bad dream."

"Yes." Her voice was still frail. She dragged her hand through her hair and trembled.

"The fire's died out." He rose and went over to the stone fireplace and began poking at the pile of gray ashes. "Let me stir things up again."

As if he hadn't already stirred things up enough, Dani thought miserably.

When she'd first escaped from Peter, Dani had suffered the terrifying nightmares every night. After a few months of therapy, she'd managed to keep them at bay for sometimes weeks at a time.

And now they'd returned. Giving her one more thing to deal with.

An ember caught and flared. Bram put another log on the fire, then turned around. Her face, in the flickering amber glow, was still too pale. And her eyes were wide, filled with lingering fear. Something was gnawing at her. Something even worse than Ryan's death. Shadows haunted her gypsy-dark eyes. And, he suspected, her heart.

"It's nothing to be ashamed about, Dani." She didn't murmur a single word of protest when he sat down beside her and put his arm around her too-stiff shoulders. "To tell you the truth, I've been having nightmares myself since the avalanche."

"Really?" His soothing touch, his reassuring voice, his solid strength were wonderfully calming.

"Really." Some errant impulse had him press his lips against the top of her head.

Bram heard her soft, rippling sigh. Felt her slender body begin to relax. He thought about the past few days, belatedly realizing that while his mother had wept and his father had turned silently inward, while he'd tried to drink himself into oblivion, Dani had remained amazingly, unflinchingly in control.

"Didn't anyone ever tell you that you don't always have to be a pillar of strength?" He felt her stiffen and realized he'd said the wrong thing.

"You're mistaken." She tilted her head back and looked directly at him. Her firm voice was far different from her earlier, frightened one. "I do."

He thought of arguing, but one look at the determination in her gaze changed his mind. When something deep inside him stirred—something that felt uncomfortably like sympathy—Bram reminded himself that even more dangerous than playing cards with a man named Doc, or eating in a place called Mom's, was messing around with a woman whose troubles were worse than your own.

He forced an uncaring shrug he did not feel. His eyes turned cool, belying the fiery passion they'd shared. "Suit yourself."

Despite her brave words, she didn't protest when he failed to move away. Instead, she put her head against his shoulder and closed her eyes.

They stayed that way the remainder of the night, lying together in front of the fire, warding off unwelcome dreams.

BY THE FOLLOWING MORNING the snow had stopped. The county snowplows were out at dawn, clearing the roads, allowing Dani and Bram to return to town.

With the morning came the return of the tension between them. As they left the cabin, their eyes met and Bram knew that Dani felt it, too.

She was wound tight. Too tight. As Bram drove along the familiar back roads, he considered doing something, anything, to ease her discomfort, then realized that his own thoughts were uncharacteristically mixed and tangled.

The morning sun cast brilliance upon the snow-dusted peaks, making them glitter like diamonds. Despite the fact that his brother had died up there in those often cruel and treacherous mountains, Bram still found them to be one of the most breathtaking sights in the world.

That they were every bit as perilous as they were beautiful only added to their attraction. The strange thing was, he had felt the same way about Dani last night. Although he'd never been one to indulge in lengthy or painful soul-searching, as he'd lain awake, watching her sleep, Bram had come to the conclusion that it was the underlying sense of danger that had made him break long-held societal and familial taboos for a forbidden night of passion with his dead brother's fiancée.

Okay. So that explained last night, Bram thought now. But God help him, in this bright and painfully sober light of day, he found himself to be experiencing that same ominous attraction.

The thing to do, he decided, was to get the hell out of town. Before he made a miserable situation even worse. For both of them.

During the drive back to town, as Bram remained silently mired in his own gritty thoughts, Dani almost managed to convince herself that she would be able to put last night behind her and pretend the scandalously fiery lovemaking had never happened.

She thought, as she and Bram exchanged stiff, awkward goodbyes, that she would probably never see Ryan's brother again.

She was soon to be proved wrong.

On both counts.

5

BELYING THE SONG LYRICS about it never raining in California, the first day of April dawned cold and wet. Oblivious to the lousy weather, Bram was running along the hard-packed sand of the beach in front of his house. Unlike the other fitness buffs who had also braved the rain to maintain their hard, California travel-poster bodies, Bram ran not for physical fitness, or to achieve any elusive runner's high.

The truth was, he was out in the early-morning fog, as he'd been every morning since Ryan's funeral, trying to outrun the demons who were chasing him. Death, grief, guilt and lust. His own personal Four Horsemen of the Apocalypse.

Every day he grieved the loss of his brother; every night he relived the horror of watching him die. Guilt that he'd not been able to save Ryan gnawed at Bram continually, ripping at his heart with its painfully sharp teeth. Bram was not all that surprised to be so tormented; it was, he suspected, a fairly normal, albeit painful part of the grieving process.

What did come as a distinct and unpleasant surprise, however, was the way Dani Cantrell had infiltrated his mind. He thought about her too much. During the day he was able to almost drive her from his mind by concentrating on the myriad problems with *Scandals*, but keeping her at bay during the long dark nights was proving impossible.

Sensual images of Dani lying in front of the fireplace, her fragrant flesh gleaming in the dancing red-and-orange light of the flames, haunted him. So much so, that even when he was with Eden, it was Dani's lips he was tasting, Dani's slender curves pressed so invitingly against his. And, heaven help him, even when he climaxed, it was Dani's warm and welcoming body he fantasized filling with his seed.

The fact that it was Eden Vail, not Dani, he'd wake up beside in the morning left Bram feeling uncharacteristically frustrated. The idea that he was suffering such vividly lustful dreams about the only woman his brother had ever loved left him feeling guilty.

And so Bram continued to run. And run. And run.

IT WAS A TYPICAL San Francisco April day. Cold and foggy. But as she drove home from her afternoon appointment, Dani remained oblivious to the rain streaming down her windshield.

She was, in a word, shell-shocked.

Lost in her tumbling, turmoiled thoughts, she parked her car and began to climb the steep steps leading to her apartment. Distracted as she was, Dani failed to see the man following her until she was at her front door.

"Hello, Dani."

The horridly familiar voice had her spinning around. "What are you doing here, Peter?" she demanded.

"Can't a man drop by to visit his wife?" His expression was falsely innocent, but Dani could see the veiled violence sparked by her unwelcoming tone.

"Ex-wife," she corrected. She turned around and managed, just barely, to get the key in the lock on the first try.

"I seem to recall the minister saying something about until death do us part." His tone was as innocuous as his expression. But Dani recognized the threat.

Her blood chilled. "I still have the restraining order," she warned. A judge friend of Ryan's had issued the order while she'd been in the hospital. For weeks she'd slept with it beneath her pillow, as if it were a talisman that could keep her from harm.

"Dani, Dani," Peter complained with a friendly, somewhat hurt smile. "You're overreacting again."

"Excuse me." She was surprised at how strong she'd become. Despite her earlier shock today, she realized she was more than capable of standing up to her former husband. "Stalkers tend to make me a little edgy."

"Is that what you think I'm doing?" Peter lifted a brow above the tortoiseshell frames of his glasses. "Stalking you?"

"It wouldn't be the first time." She was already tired of this conversation. "It's also against the law." She turned away again, intending to go inside.

He put his hand on her elbow. Dani immediately shook off his touch. "Honestly, Dani, I was across the street in the pub, having a beer and watching the Giants game on TV, when I glanced outside and saw you parking your car.

"Since I've been feeling bad about what happened between us, I thought I'd just take the opportunity to offer my condolences regarding your recent shock."

At first Dani thought he was referring to this morning's bombshell. Then she realized he was talking about Ryan's death.

"That's very kind of you." She didn't believe him for a minute. "I appreciate your concern." Peter wasn't the only one who could lie. "Now, if you don't mind, I really would like to get out of this rain."

Fury at being so summarily dismissed flashed in his eyes, but his smile remained friendly. "Sure." Without asking permission, he reached out and ran the back of a leather-glove-clad hand down her cheek. "Take care, sweetheart. And just remember, if there's anything you ever need—"

His touch still possessed the power to terrorize. Dani couldn't hide her shudder. "I don't need anything from you, Peter." She opened the door and quickly darted inside.

Before she could slam the door in his handsome face, Peter got in the last word. "I'll be thinking of you."

With that threat ringing in her ears, Dani shut the door and fastened all three locks. She made her way to the couch, sank down onto the chintz cushions, buried her face in her hands and began to tremble.

BRAM'S OFFICE BUNGALOW, located at the far reaches of Eclipse Studios' sprawling properties, belied his international fame and fortune. Rather than the ego-gratifying, overwhelming structure Dani would have expected, it proved to be a small white stucco building devoid of any outer decoration save for a small sign, reading Fortune Productions, beside the door.

As the golf cart carrying Dani to her destination approached the building, the door opened. Dani was not surprised to find Bram waiting for her. She'd been detained by the elderly studio guard until Bram, contacted by phone, had given whatever magic command opened those high wrought-iron gates to visitors.

Bram inclined his head. Briefly. "Hello, Dani." There wasn't a hint of welcome in his tone. His voice, and his expression, remained unnervingly neutral. "This is a surprise."

If you think this is a surprise, just wait, she thought.

It had been six weeks since Ryan's funeral. Six long and nerve-racking weeks, during which time she'd tried to convince herself that the effect Bramwell Fortune had had on her emotions had been a transitory response to her grief and confusion.

She had told herself that, over and over again. She'd spent the past forty-eight hours steeling herself for this meeting. But she realized now, as she looked at him framed in the doorway, that she'd badly miscalculated. His dark blue eyes were narrowed against the sun, making them unreadable. One tanned hand was braced on the doorjamb, the other thrust deep in the front pocket of a pair of black jeans. The seemingly casual gesture drew Dani's gaze downward, to where the denim cupped his sex. The memory of the way he'd felt against her—inside her—caused heat to curl in her belly.

As she climbed out of the cart, Dani blew out a soft, steadying breath. Her nerves, which were already strung far too tightly for comfort, began to unravel. Although she'd never actually believed in the phenomenon, her legs suddenly felt unreasonably wobbly, as if she were attempting to stand on the deck of a storm-tossed sloop.

"Hello, Bram." Her voice was soft and hesitant. It was, she thought with a burst of self-directed temper, a stranger's voice.

Her voice was warm and sweet, like the café au lait Bram liked to drink in New Orleans's French Quarter. It was a lushly female voice that brought to mind steamy nights and rumpled sheets.

He'd been taunted by that voice for weeks, waking after arousing dreams of Dani wrapped around him—all tight and wet and so very, very hot.

Tension was crackling inside Dani like a downed electrical wire in a thunderstorm. Though Bram's pose remained relaxed, there was a coiled, wound intensity about him that frightened her.

And if there was one thing Dani had vowed she would never—ever!—allow, it was to permit any man to frighten her again. She squared her shoulders. Her fingers tightened around the leather strap of her purse.

"I hope I haven't interrupted your work."

Bram watched her struggle for control and wondered if she realized that stiffening her spine that way only succeeded in causing her breasts to press seductively against the crimson silk of her blouse.

Her short white skirt—styled like the sarong Dorothy Lamour made famous in *Road to Singapore*—displayed an enticing amount of slender leg. Bram remembered all too well exactly how those long legs had felt, wrapped around his hips.

"Don't worry." He shrugged. "You haven't interrupted anything that can't wait." He moved aside. "Come on in."

Dani hadn't known what exactly to expect of Bram's office interior. Sleek sophisticated ebony, brass and glass, perhaps. Or innately masculine—lots of red cordovan leather and dark paneling, like that found in a turn-of-the-century men's club.

But instead, it was bright and casual and inviting. White walls showcased a remarkable collection of antique movie posters. One poster depicted Clark Gable and Charles Laughton's memorable clash from *Mutiny on the Bounty;* another captured Rita Hayworth's dazzling image in *Blood and Sand*.

A trio of old-fashioned pinball machines lined one wall, a soda fountain with a gleaming brass railing and red-and-white-striped bar stools took up a corner of the office, while a pool table claimed the center of the floor. "I saw some picketers outside the gates," she said in an attempt at small talk. "I got the impression they're not thrilled about your latest film."

Bram's mouth drew into a tight, angry line. "They were out there when I got back from Tahoe City. What the idiots are too damn stupid to realize is all they're doing is creating a lot of prerelease hype, which will help boost ratings when the miniseries does air."

"So you're not dropping the project?" She'd seen a recent report on "Entertainment Tonight" suggesting he might.

"And let a few loudmouthed crackpots dictate my creative vision? Hell, no. No more than you'd let anyone tell you what pictures to paint."

"Good point," she murmured, remembering the way Peter had derided her creative efforts.

Her wandering glance settled on a nearby table. On top of the table rested an oversize helmet—a great deal like the one Darth Vader wore in the *Star Wars* films. But even larger.

"Is that what I think it is?"

"A virtual reality helmet," Bram agreed. "You'll have to give it a shot. It's a lot like an E-ticket ride on the starship *Enterprise*."

That's all she needed—something to make her head spin more than it already was. Despite her nervousness, Dani smiled. "So it's true what they say."

For not the first time since their enforced time together, they proved to be on the same wavelength. "About the only difference between men and boys being the price of their toys?" Bram supplied. "Absolutely."

He waved his hand toward a sofa covered in a cheery red, gold and green print resembling a Navajo blanket. "Have a seat. Would you like a drink? Or something from the fountain? I make a pretty mean chocolate soda."

"No, thank you." Her stomach was already twisted into knots. Her legs still uncharacteristically unstable, she lowered herself gratefully onto the sofa.

"So, to what do I owe this visit?"

When she nervously dragged an unsteady hand through her hair, Bram noticed, with his director's eye for detail, that she was still wearing her engagement ring.

"It's a long story."

He picked up a pack of cigarettes from the desk, shook one out, planted it in the corner of his mouth and lit it. "I'm not going anywhere," he said on a plume of blue smoke that wafted her way.

The smoke proved her undoing. Dani's stomach instantly revolted.

"Where's the bathroom?" she managed as she lurched to her feet. Her purse dropped to the floor.

Her snowy complexion had turned nearly as green as the felt topping on the pool table. A warning tolled in Bram's mind.

"First door to the right."

She literally staggered out of the room like a drunk on a two-week bender. Bram considered going to her, heard the sound of water running, and decided she'd be all right on her own.

He ground out the cigarette. As he nuked a cup of water for tea in the microwave, his mind latched on to the single, most probable reason for Dani's unexpected arrival here today.

He'd bet his last Oscar that she was pregnant.

The $64,000 question was, was the baby Ryan's?

Or his?

When she finally exited the bathroom, her complexion was wraith pale. Her red-rimmed eyes were exhausted.

"Here." He took her arm, led her across the room to the couch. "Feeling better?"

She did. Not much. But a little. Mostly she was humiliated. Embarrassed color rose in her cheeks and all she could manage was a little nod.

"You don't have to be embarrassed in front of me, Dani." Bram was surprised by how fragile she looked. She reminded him of a piece of fine porcelain about to crack.

Her pallor moved something elemental deep inside him. Something unbidden. And not entirely welcome.

He steeped a tea bag in the hot water and tossed in a sugar cube. "After all, we've been about as intimate as two people can be." He placed a plate of English water crackers on the pine table in front of the sofa.

"That's what I've come to discuss with you," Dani admitted as she accepted the cup of tea. Since it was too hot to drink and she still didn't trust her mutinous stomach, she placed it

on the table. She did, however, take a tentative nibble of one
of the crackers.

"I thought it might be." He leaned back against his desk,
legs crossed at the ankles, arms folded in front of his chest.

Stalling for time, she picked up the cup and ran her finger
around the rim. "I don't exactly know where to begin."

"Normally, when someone's pitching me a story, I suggest
they begin at the beginning. But in our case, I think you can
just cut to the chase." His voice remained mild but an arrogant glint shone in his eyes. "And I'd suggest you drop the shy,
tongue-tied-maiden role." He ignored her sudden, angry intake of breath. "It doesn't suit you."

Dani had no way of knowing that he'd purposely made
her angry in order to shock her back into her usual feisty self.
All she knew was that his sarcastic tone touched off her temper. Irritation flowed hotly through her blood, burning away
her earlier nervousness.

"All right." She tilted her chin again, met his gaze straight
on and crossed her legs with an enticing swish of silk on silk.
"I'm pregnant."

"Somehow, that doesn't surprise me."

"Well, that makes one of us."

"Is it Ryan's?"

A lie would have been the prudent thing. The safe thing.
But perhaps it was Bram's piercing dark blue gaze, or perhaps it was something else that made her tell the truth.

"No. The baby's yours, Bram."

"I may have been drunk that night but I definitely remember you saying the next morning that you were on the Pill."

"I was." The question she saw in his eyes was one of the
reasons she'd dreaded telling him about the pregnancy. Dani
dragged a hand through her thick hair. "But somehow, during all the rush of wedding preparations, I forgot to take a pill.
Then I missed a second one the night of the avalanche."

Bram nodded. "Makes sense to me."

How could he be so damn calm about this? Dani wondered. She'd been absolutely frantic, counting back the days, waiting—praying!—for a period that had never come.

She decided that the obvious answer was that Bram Fortune was one of those Stone Age males who simply considered an unplanned pregnancy the woman's problem.

"Wedding plans probably would distract anyone," Bram agreed. "As for the day of the avalanche, you were obviously distraught," he continued in that same rational tone she was beginning to hate. "It stands to reason that something as ordinary as taking a little pink pill would slip your mind."

"That's exactly what happened."

She took a tentative sip of tea. It was hot and sweet and, along with the crackers, was just what her stomach needed.

"I've always believed in taking full responsibility for my actions," she said.

Bram nodded. "I seem to recall a youthful excursion to Squaw Valley. When Ryan tried to take the blame and you wouldn't let him."

"I didn't come here to talk about Ryan."

"Fine." A white line circled his lips at the mention of his brother's name.

A fleeting emotion that could have been anger—or pain— flashed in Bram's eyes, come and gone so quickly that if she hadn't been observing him carefully, Dani would have missed it.

"This is your script." He picked up the pack of cigarettes again, recalled her condition, and returned it to the table. "Go on."

Dani took a deep breath. "The ultrasound puts me at six weeks."

"Not to muddy the waters with technical medical details, but I've written the triangle story of a woman and two men before," Bram said. "In *Tarnished Vows*. And I seem to recall from my research that sperm have a way of sticking around a few days."

"A few days," Dani allowed. "But not a month."

Bram couldn't conceal his surprise. "A month? Are you saying that you and Ryan hadn't had sex for a month before he died?" Disbelief practically dripped from his tone.

"I'm saying we hadn't *made love* for a month before he died." It was important to Dani to stress that what she and Ryan had shared was a deep and everlasting love. While what she'd experienced with his brother had been merely lust.

If he picked up on the correction, Bram ignored it. "Whose crazy idea was that?"

"Actually, it was mine," Dani admitted. She'd waited so long to be Ryan's wife. She'd wanted their wedding night to be special. Memorable. Romantic. As foolish as it now sounded, she'd wanted to pretend that they'd be making love for the very first time. Which was why abstinence for the month prior to their marriage had seemed to make a certain amount of sense.

"And Ryan went along with that?"

"Of course." They both knew that Ryan Fortune had never denied Dani anything.

"Lord." Bram shook his head in blatant disbelief. "Obviously my baby brother was even more of a saint than I knew."

"Whatever you think of our personal decision, it means that there's no way Ryan could be the father of my baby."

She pressed her hand against her stomach, as if to protect her unborn child from his father's burning gaze. How she wished that it *was* Ryan's child she was carrying!

Dani bit her lip as she shook off the painful thought. "You don't have to worry, Bram. I have no intention of forcing you into doing anything you don't want to do."

His eyes narrowed. "You're not thinking about an abortion."

"No." She shook her head. "Although I never would have planned this pregnancy, having considered all the options, I've decided to have my baby."

"*Our* baby," Bram corrected quietly.

"I'm not asking for child support." She was twisting her engagement ring around and around. "After all, my work is beginning to sell quite well." The words tumbled out. "At least, well enough to support my baby. Believe it or not, I actually seem to have developed a following, and . . ."

As Bram's quiet interjection belatedly sank in, Dani's words drifted off. "What did you say?"

"You keep saying *my* baby. I merely pointed out that you're pregnant with *our* child."

"Oh." Dani took another deep breath that did nothing to instill calm. "Well." She absently began twisting the ring again. "The bottom line is that I want my—I mean, *our*—baby, Bram. More than I ever would have thought possible."

Her dark eyes were earnest. And determined. Bram could tell that this was no spur-of-the-moment decision. She'd obviously thought it through. The only thing she'd neglected to factor in was his own feelings on the matter.

"I can see that."

He remembered, with painful clarity, sitting with Ryan on the deck of his house, listening to his brother wax poetic about his planned life with Dani. There would be children, Ryan had proclaimed. Just as they had always agreed about everything else, both Dani and Ryan had yearned for a large, loving family.

Bram thought how thrilled Ryan would undoubtedly have been by Dani's news. He thought about his brother asking him to be not only his best man at his and Dani's wedding, but also godfather to their firstborn child. And Bram knew what he must do.

"Well." Dani exhaled a ragged breath. Breaking the news to Bram hadn't been as difficult as she'd feared. Perhaps she'd misjudged him. Just a little.

"Thank you for being so understanding, Bram. And now that we've had this little discussion, I'll let you get back to work." Dani stood, prepared to make her escape.

"Don't you want to know how I feel about all this?"

"Oh." She stared up at him, wishing she could tell what he was thinking. But the simple truth was that this man she'd made a child with was little more than a stranger. "Of course." Her wary tone suggested otherwise.

"Fine. In the first place," he said, ticking his thoughts off on his fingers, "I intend to pay your expenses."

"But, I told you, that's not—"

"I know what you told me. But you're not exactly Picasso yet, sweetheart. And it takes a lot of money to support a child."

He'd do his duty, Bram decided. To Dani. And, more important, to Ryan. He'd accept the responsibility of this child. But God, the cost was high!

Dani watched emotion darken his eyes and wished, not for the first time, that she could tell what he was thinking.

"All right," she agreed, thinking of her dwindling bank balance. The expenses she'd already incurred had been higher than she'd imagined. Who would have guessed that prenatal vitamins could be so expensive? "You can help out."

Lord, she could be maddening! Bram wondered how Ryan had thought he was going to handle this woman. "Thank you," he said dryly, fully intending to do a lot more than help out.

"Well, then, if that's settled—"

"I'm not quite finished."

"Excuse me." She sat back down, crossed her long legs, and lifted her chin a defiant notch. "Continue."

She inclined her head in a haughty way that would have done a deposed Russian czarina proud. Bram could practically see the jeweled tiara perched atop her gleaming jet hair.

"Very good." He nodded his approval at her performance. "Bette Davis playing the Virgin Queen. With just a hint of Garbo as Anna Christie tossed in for sex appeal. If you ever decide to try acting, let me know. I'll arrange a screen test."

"How very kind. But I think I'll pass."

Bram shrugged even as he vowed to get that remarkable face on film. "Suit yourself."

He was looking at her with a narrow-eyed, unblinking stare that gave her the impression he was measuring her through the lens of a camera. Dani decided the time had come to drag this conversational train back to its original track.

"I believe you had something else to say? About my pregnancy?"

Once again he gave her points for what his father would have called "good old-fashioned gumption."

"I don't want our son or daughter growing up knowing only one of its parents."

Dani thought she'd carefully weighed all the possibilities. This was one option she hadn't considered. "Are you saying—?"

"I'll want to be involved in our child's life."

"Oh." It wouldn't be so bad, she mused. Weekend visits from time to time, the occasional summer holiday. And besides, Bram was one of Hollywood's most eligible bachelors. Hadn't *People* magazine recently voted him the Sexiest Man of the Year?

How long would Bram Fortune remain interested in playing part-time daddy? Not long at all, Dani reassured herself.

"I suppose I wouldn't have a problem granting paternal visitation rights."

"You still don't get it, do you?"

"Get what?"

"I have no intention of being an every-other-Saturday, afternoon-at-the-zoo kind of father, Dani."

Her stomach clenched. A headache began pounding at her temple.

"What, exactly, are you suggesting, Bram?"

"I'd think that you should be able to see that there's only one logical way to handle this."

Dani's palms broke into a sweat. "What's that?"

"Isn't it obvious?" His answering smile was a wolfish slash of white. A predator's smile. "We have to get married."

6

"MARRIED?"

The single word came out in a croak. "As in you and I?"

Dani stared at Bram, desperately seeking some sign of amusement at her expense. Her dark eyes had grown wide and luminous, reminding Bram of a startled doe captured by a pair of blinding headlights.

He glanced around the room. "See any other two people in here?"

"But we don't even like each other."

"We managed to like each other well enough to screw each other's brains out the night of my brother's funeral."

Dani flinched. "That never should have happened."

"Probably not. But it did. Now we have to behave like grown-ups and face the consequences."

"But—"

"Look, Dani, the way I see it, we took a stupid chance. And we lost. Big time. So the only thing to do is pay up."

"That is undoubtedly the most unromantic proposal any woman ever received."

"It's not exactly a romantic situation, sweetheart," he countered.

She folded her arms across her chest and glared at him. "Finally. Something we agree on."

"Need I remind you that it's my child you're carrying?" His tone remained mild but danger lurked in his glittering gaze, reminding Dani that this was an individual accustomed to getting his own way. *Tough*, she decided.

"That's not necessary. Since I have a vivid reminder of it every morning when I'm on my knees in front of the toilet."

Bram swore under his breath. Then he sat down beside her and took both her hands in his. They were ice-cold, revealing that she was not as self-possessed as she was trying to appear.

"Look, Dani, it's important to me that my name be listed as the father on our child's birth certificate."

"You certainly don't have to marry me to achieve that."

"True enough. But what makes you think I'd allow any child of mine to suffer the stigma of illegitimacy?"

"This is Hollywood," she stated unnecessarily. She tugged at her hands, which were still captured in his. "No one worries about things like that here."

"Perhaps not here," he allowed. Bram tightened his hold, not yet ready to release her. Familiar with her quicksilver temper, he wasn't about to let her march out of his office before they settled things.

To his satisfaction, of course. Bram Fortune would have it no other way.

"But believe me, Dani, I realize this fantasyland I live and work in is not the real world. And I hate the idea of our child's status ending up splashed all over the front pages of the tabloids."

She had to admit Bram had a point. The idea of total strangers reading all about her private life—the details of which were bound to be, at best, exaggerations, at worst, out-and-out lies—was unthinkable.

If she were the only one involved, Dani knew she could tough it out. But there was an innocent baby to consider. An infant who would come into this world branded with the stigma of his parents' sin.

She tried to tell herself that given time, the rumors, the scandal, would die out. But she knew that wasn't really the case. Because just as there were unscrupulous, so-called reporters willing to traffic in others' personal misfortunes and tragedies, there would also always be those eager to read— and believe—the whispers and innuendos.

Someday, when she'd least expect it, the story, and the resultant pain, would be resurrected. She squeezed her eyes shut at the unsavory prospect. Oh, she could take it, Dani assured herself again. Her brutal time with Peter, and its healing aftermath, had proved that she was, after all, a survivor. They could throw all the filthy mud at her they wanted.

But the one thing Dani knew she could never bear was the thought of any of it touching her child.

"Those aren't exactly the type of press clippings a mother envisions pasting into a baby book," she murmured.

A little silence settled over them. Bram was the first to break it. "So, what do you say?"

Dani wondered how many women in America would literally kill to receive a proposal from the rich and famous, not to mention devastatingly sexy, Bram Fortune.

"There's something you should know before I give you my answer."

"This is where you tell me you don't love me."

"It's nothing against you personally. It's just that—"

"You still love Ryan."

"Yes." Even hearing her beloved's name tore at the ragged edges of her still-shattered heart.

"So?"

"Why would you want to marry me, knowing I love your brother? That I'll always love him?"

"Ryan's dead," Bram reminded grimly.

"Still—"

"Look, I'll make a deal with you."

Dani looked at him warily. The man was full of surprises today; she honestly didn't know how many more she could take. "What kind of deal?"

"We'll get married, you'll have a respectable, legitimate pregnancy. Then, after the baby is born, we'll get divorced. That way, everyone wins."

As she thought through Bram's surprising proposition, her gaze idly circled the room, coming to land on a silver-framed photo of Eden Vail, her voluptuous body crowded into a beaded gold minidress so tight it looked as if the gorgeous blond actress had been dipped into a vat of gilt paint.

"What about her?"

Bram followed the direction of Dani's gaze. "Eden isn't your problem," he said dismissively.

Dani lifted a brow. "So she *is* a problem?"

Did the woman have to argue every little point? "What Eden and I share has nothing to do with us."

Dani could see the No Trespassing signs going up around Bram. His face closed up, like a window being shuttered before a storm. His eyes once again turned frustratingly inscrutable.

"I read she lives with you."

"You read wrong. She has her own place in Beverly Hills. Though she has been known to spend the weekend at my place," he allowed.

"Do you plan to continue seeing her?"

"It would be a bit difficult not to continue seeing Eden, since she's starring in my current picture," he stated dryly. "But if what you really mean is do I plan to continue sleeping with Eden after our marriage, the answer is *no*.

"Trust me, Dani, the day this picture wraps, whatever relationship Eden Vail and I share would have been over, anyway."

"That sounds suspiciously like the old casting-couch routine." Dani didn't bother to keep the scorn from her voice. "Tell me, Bram, is that how you get such brilliant performances from your female stars? By sleeping with them during the filming?"

"In some cases it doesn't hurt." He surprised her by answering honestly.

"And then you dump them after the wrap party?"

"Actually, if there's going to be any dumping done, you're looking at the potential dumpee. Because Eden's emotionally already on her way to her next film. And her next affair."

The little telltale signs had become obvious since he'd returned from Tahoe City. Only last night, she'd canceled dinner with him in order to read for a part with a producer at Columbia Pictures. This morning, when she showed up for work on the set—late as usual—the makeup woman had complained about Eden's unattractive beard burn.

"Our marriage will just move the time clock forward a little."

Dani wondered what type of man Bram was that he could be so remarkably cavalier about the end of a relationship. The kind of man, she reminded herself, who could actually suggest an empty sham of a marriage.

"Where would we live?" she asked, thinking of the lovely Russian Hill home she and Ryan had planned to move into.

Bram glanced around the office. "Since my work is here, it'd be a bit difficult for me to relocate to San Francisco." He hoped Dani wouldn't prove difficult about this point. "If you're worried about having a place to paint, there's plenty of room in my beach house for a studio. And the light's terrific."

"What would be wrong with my remaining in San Francisco?" she argued. "While you stay here?"

"How about the little fact that our living apart would inspire all sorts of gossip? It's important to our child that everyone—especially those unholy vipers at the tabloids—believe ours is a real marriage."

Once again, Dani gave Bram reluctant points for how quickly he'd managed to consider all the aspects of his proposed marriage. But still . . .

Almost as much as entering into a marriage that was both a lie and a farce, Dani hated the idea of leaving the city she'd come to love.

On the other hand, she mused, there were so many memories there: memories of her disastrous marriage to Peter, of her hopeful, blissful time with Ryan. Perhaps a change would do her some good.

And, although she hated to admit it, after having Peter show up at her door the other day, the prospect of moving nearly four hundred miles away from her ex-husband had its own appeal.

"I suppose you're right." She sounded, Bram noted, less than enthusiastic. He was not pleased by her next question. Neither was he all that surprised. "What about sex?"

"What about it?"

"Since it would only be a marriage of convenience, I don't think we should complicate things any more than they already are by sleeping together."

With effort, Bram refrained from pointing out that if they'd stuck to sleeping that night in the cabin, there wouldn't be a need for this marriage in the first place.

Instead, he rubbed his chin and considered her reservation for a long, silent time. "I'm not going to lie and say that I won't want you, Dani," he said finally. "But I will give you my word not to do anything you don't want me to do."

Dani wished his agreement hadn't carried such a dangerous caveat. Try as she might, she'd not been able to forget Bram's thrilling lovemaking.

Ignoring the little voice of caution trying to make itself heard in the far reaches of her mind, Dani made her decision.

"All right," she agreed without enthusiasm. "I'll marry you, Bram."

"Thank you." Bram's full lips twisted into a mirthless line that only an extremely charitable person could have called a smile. He stood. "So. Where's your luggage?"

"I don't have any. I'd planned on returning home to San Francisco tonight."

"No problem. We can buy whatever you need in Las Vegas."

"Las Vegas?"

His eyes narrowed, reminding her once again that Bram was not a man to be crossed. "You did just agree to marry me."

"Yes, but—"

"So, the way I see it, there's no point in waiting."

"But, to run off this way, without telling anyone . . ."

Her voice drifted off. She dragged her hands through her hair in confusion. She looked exhausted and overwhelmed and still too pale. Bram felt his heart going out to her. She'd been carrying this burden alone too long. All the more reason to get matters settled as quickly as possible.

"Surely you weren't planning on another big ceremony with all the bells and whistles?"

"Of course not." She began nervously twisting her engagement ring again. "Actually," she said, "I wasn't planning any wedding when I came here today."

Dani was tired. Her stomach was, at best, still iffy. And her head ached. "It's too soon," she murmured, rubbing at her temple, where the headache she'd been fighting all day continued to build.

He saw the gesture and felt a brief prick of conscience. Bram knew he was rushing her. But, dammit, he didn't see where they had much choice.

"Look, Dani," he began again, mustering every bit of hard-won patience he possessed, "I'm flying to Thailand tomorrow to film on location for three weeks. I'm already behind schedule and over budget. I can't reschedule an entire crew."

"Then, don't." She tilted her chin at him in that pugnacious gesture he was beginning to hate. "As it happens, I have a show scheduled here in town in three weeks."

"I didn't know that."

She shrugged. "There wasn't any reason for you to know. But as it happens, you're not the only one behind schedule. I promised Arturo I'd have twenty-five canvases completed. And I'm still three short."

"Arturo?" A big-screen image immediately came to mind. Ricardo Montalban in his younger years, perhaps. Dark and sexy, the Latin-lover type women seemed to find irresistible.

"Arturo Rodriguez. He has a gallery in West Hollywood." Bram's eyes narrowed. "I've never heard of him." He made a mental note to have the guy checked out.

His suspicious tone rankled. Dani refrained from sarcastically asking whether Bram was personally familiar with every gallery owner in Los Angeles.

"I'm not surprised," she said instead, "since Arturo's relatively new in town. He moved here from Santa Fe, with a brief stop in San Francisco, where he had a little place in Cow Hollow. He had some success with a few of my earlier works and thought I might enjoy a chance to expand my horizons."

Dani had wanted to cancel the show after Ryan's death but Arturo had argued that immersing herself in her work might help her overcome her pain. His strategy had worked. Somewhat.

There were days, as she was struggling desperately to meet the demanding deadline, when hours would go by without her thinking of Ryan. And of what might have been.

"So," she said, "the obvious thing to do is for you to keep to your schedule and for me to keep to mine. Then, after we've both fulfilled our obligations, we can discuss setting a date."

Bram was not about to go off to the Thai jungles without this issue firmly resolved. He knew he had a reputation for being ruthless. Personally, he'd always seen himself as determined. Whether he was after a hotly sought-after screenplay or a woman, his methodology was always the same. He would carefully plot his strategy, then stick to it unwaveringly, achieving success in the end.

Unfortunately, nothing about Dani had gone according to plan.

"You realize," he drawled, unable to resist giving it one last parting shot, "that the longer you wait, the more advanced in your pregnancy you'll be for the ceremony."

"Don't worry, Bram," she assured him silkily, knowing what he was doing and refusing to bend to his will. "I promise not to embarrass you by waddling down the aisle mere hours before delivery."

Bram's eyes made a slow, judicial perusal of her body, lingering over her breasts, which seemed more voluptuous. Her waist was still wasp slender, her stomach flat.

"I don't embarrass all that easily. And believe it or not, sweetheart, the idea of you large with my child is proving more and more appealing."

From the gleam in his eyes, Dani could almost believe that Bram Fortune was experiencing something akin to male pride at the idea of having planted his seed.

"Men," she muttered. But her tone lacked its earlier censorious edge and her gaze softened.

"I know." Color had risen in her cheeks like a misty summer sunrise. Unable to resist the lure of her pink-tinged skin, he ran the back of his hand down the side of her face. "Can't live with us." Around her jaw. When his thumb brushed against her lips, they parted on a soft, surprised intake of breath. "Can't murder us."

He was smiling at her. A friendly, easy smile that belied the warmth rising in his midnight blue eyes.

Dani backed away. Physically and emotionally. "Dammit, Bram—"

She put her hand on his chest, intending to push him away. Seemingly unperturbed, he covered her hand with his. "If it's only a marriage of convenience," he said, reminding her of her own earlier description, "then we may as well get the bureaucratic paperwork over with."

"Lord, you're so romantic," she complained. "How can I refuse?"

"You want romance?" He lifted her hand to his lips. "Marry me, Dani." His eyes didn't move from hers as he kissed each fingertip in turn. "Be my wife." The feathery touch of his smiling lips was making her skin tingle. "Let me make an honest woman of you."

Once again his chauvinistic words almost caused her temper to flare. Once again, just in time, she realized he was teasing.

"I need to think."

"You can think on the plane." He turned her hand over and pressed a kiss against the sensitive skin of her palm. Although she knew it was her imagination, Dani could have sworn she felt her flesh sizzle. "On the way to Vegas."

Her mind was floating. His caress was making her knees weak. Struggling against the tender web he was weaving around them, Dani chose to blame the dizzying feelings on her pregnancy.

"Do you always get everything you want?" Her tone was half teasing, half accusation.

"No." He dropped her hand as if it had suddenly turned hot. While he, in contrast, had turned cold. "I don't."

Their eyes met. Their thoughts tangled and Dani knew that once again they were sharing the same thought.

Ryan. She found it ironic that less than two months ago, she'd been the impulsive one, living solely for the moment, about to marry a man who carefully planned out every aspect of his life.

And now, she was the one struggling to be practical. Perhaps, she mused, it was impending motherhood that had her needing to be certain that she was making the right choice. Because whatever decision she made would involve not only herself, but an innocent child.

"If you're waiting for an ironclad, money-back guarantee that this is the absolutely best decision under the circumstances, I can't give it to you."

Bram's deep voice broke into her thoughts, once again revealing his uncanny ability to read her mind. "But I do promise that I'll never do anything to make you regret your choice."

During their brief time together, she and Bram had shared more than passion. Alone with their grief, they'd shared a part of themselves she suspected not many people ever witnessed. And although she hated to admit it, Bram was proving to be an honorable man.

Even so, Dani was already regretting the decision she knew she was about to make.

"I give up." On a frustrated huff of breath, she surrendered, as she'd suspected all along that she would. "You're right. Let's get it over with."

7

IT WAS DEFINITELY NOT the lovely ceremony Dani had planned with Ryan. And it was worlds different from her glamorous Monte Carlo elopement.

Mere hours after her arrival at Eclipse Studios, she found herself repeating her marriage vows in front of a minister who didn't bother to conceal his boredom with a ceremony he'd done too many times to count.

"If you feel up to it, we'd better get back to L.A.," Bram said as they exited the chapel into the neon-brightened night. He'd kept the chartered jet waiting at the executive terminal.

His expression was not that of a man who'd just sworn a lifetime of love. What Dani had no way of knowing was that Bram's glower was directed inward. As a director, he was angry with himself for not having set a more romantic scene.

"Actually, if you don't mind, I'd prefer returning directly to San Francisco. All my things are there," she reminded him.

"Fine." Of course, there wouldn't be a honeymoon. Bram reminded himself that even if Dani was eager to return to his Malibu home with him, he wouldn't be there. Because he was scheduled to begin shooting in some godforsaken jungle. "I'll send you back to the city on the jet."

"What about you? Don't you have to leave for Thailand in a few hours?"

"No problem. I'll take a commercial flight home and catch up with the crew at the international terminal at LAX."

"Really, Bram, that's not necessary. I'll fly commercial."

"I'm not going to have you crowded into some flying cattle car. In case you've forgotten, Dani, you're pregnant."

How could she have forgotten? Even if her uneasy stomach wasn't constantly reminding her, she was all too aware that had it not been for their child, they wouldn't be here together in Las Vegas in the first place.

"The definitive term is *pregnant*," she told him. "That doesn't make me an invalid, Bram. In lots of countries, women work in the fields up until the moment of delivery."

Not *his* woman, Bram thought. He found himself struck with the impractical urge to lock Dani away in a protective glass bubble for the next seven months.

"Isn't it nice that you're not some Third World field hand." He looped his arm possessively around her shoulder and walked her toward the long black limo waiting at the curb. "Don't argue with me on this one, Dani. Because you won't win."

Dani's frustrated breath ruffled her dark bangs. "Has anyone ever told you that you're incredibly bossy?"

"Actually, that's one of the more flattering descriptions," he admitted easily. "And believe me, sweetheart, I try my best to live up to the image."

"Oh, hell," she huffed. "Do whatever you want."

"I always have," Bram assured her.

Dani was both relieved and vaguely disappointed when Bram didn't try to talk her into returning to L.A. with him on the twenty-minute drive to the airport.

Instead, he spent the time explaining how "his people," as he referred to them, would be arriving in San Francisco to move her belongings into his home.

A part of her wanted to object to his heavy-handedness. Another, stronger part, decided that she wasn't up to fighting what she suspected would be a losing cause. Besides, she'd always hated packing. It would be nice to simply sit back and allow someone else to do all the work.

She thought about relocating to a town she'd only briefly visited, moving into a home she'd never seen, living with a husband she barely knew. About giving birth to a child she certainly hadn't planned.

So many changes, Dani mused, as the car pulled into the terminal area. It was as if she'd suddenly been ripped away from everything familiar—like Dorothy caught up in the throes of that tornado—and plunked down in Oz. They'd called Bram's parents from the plane on the flight to Las Vegas, and although the Fortunes had expressed pleasure that Dani was pregnant with their first grandchild, their surprise and confusion at the news that their elder son was the father was more than a little apparent. Emotionally wrung out, Dani was grateful when her new in-laws didn't press for details.

As they exited the limo and approached the private jet parked on the tarmac, Dani was priding herself on having made it through the strange, unsettling day.

"Well, I suppose I'll see you in three weeks," Dani said as they stood at the bottom of the portable stairs leading to the cabin door. For some reason, she was suddenly loath to get on the plane.

"Count on it." Bram was not yet ready to let her go. He thought about convincing her to go to Thailand with him and reluctantly decided that even if she didn't have her own work to complete, the trip could prove too physically demanding. There was also the fact that his rigorous shooting schedule allowed no time for a proper honeymoon.

Dear Lord, he was looking at her that way again! Bram's intense gaze was a sensual, visual caress that excited even as it confused.

Unnerved, Dani dipped her head and drew in the fragrance of the white-rose bouquet Bram had insisted on buying her. A soft breeze feathered her hair, concealing her face.

"Dani." Unwilling to send her off without at least staking his claim on his new bride, Bram tilted her face upward with the tenderest touch of a finger beneath her chin. "Look at me."

His eyes were as dark as midnight. In the center of them a flame as white-hot as the brightest star blazed. Heat shimmied up Dani's spine. She stood still, transfixed.

He framed her face in his hands. "It suddenly occurs to me that I made a mistake back there at the chapel."

It was occurring to Dani that he wasn't the only one. She'd managed to convince herself on the flight to Las Vegas that she'd be able to keep her distance—both physical and emotional—from Bram Fortune.

But now, as she felt herself getting lost in those dark, dangerous eyes, she was forced to wonder if their forbidden night of passion in the cabin was really the anomaly she had tried so hard to convince herself it was.

"What mistake was that?" Her faint voice sounded as if it were coming from the bottom of a well.

"I got the impression that when the minister pronounced us man and wife, you didn't really want me to kiss the bride."

"I didn't." Dani waited for the bolt of lightning to come out of the star-spangled desert sky and strike her for telling such a blatant lie. Actually, she'd been disappointed by Bram's polite, subdued peck on her cheek.

"That's what you say." His voice was as hot and dark as the night. His tone suggested he knew otherwise. Bram lowered his head until his mouth was a mere whisper from hers. "But as we've already determined, my dear wife, I always get what I want. So . . ."

Dani held her breath.

Waiting. And, heaven help her, wanting.

She read the promise of seduction in his eyes.

He viewed reluctant temptation in hers.

Their lips touched.

And at that dazzling, glorious, suspended moment in time, the lightning Dani feared struck.

He tasted the same. Yet excitingly different.

His touch, his kiss, was as devastating as it had been the first time. But now, as his hands skimmed over her body and his mouth drank lustily of hers, Dani experienced a shock of wondrously passionate recognition.

His sandpaper-rough day-old beard scraped against her face. His hands tangled painfully, possessively in her hair, holding her prisoner to his intoxicating kiss.

Restraint wasn't necessary. Immersed in a rising passion that was spreading through her like wildfire, Dani could not have moved if she'd wanted to.

Which she didn't.

The lightning flashed again, closer this time.

Thunder rumbled in the distance.

Was it really thunder? Bram wondered as his tongue slid between her parted lips, stroking, exploring, savoring. Or was it the harsh, out-of-control beat of his heart?

A throaty moan escaped Dani's lips as she responded with equal fervor. Her tongue tangled sinuously with his. Her slender hands gathered up fistfuls of his shirt. On her left hand, the plain gold band that had replaced her diamond engagement ring gleamed in the streaming moonlight.

Groaning his need, Bram splayed one hand across the small of her arched back, then lower, cupping her buttocks, urging her tighter against his aching erection, marveling in some distant corner of his mind at how perfectly she fit.

Need swirled around them like a torrid desert scirocco. God help him, it was happening all over again. Bram knew it was madness to want any woman the way he wanted Dani. He knew it was insanity to *need* any woman the way he needed her.

But just as he'd done that fateful night in the cabin, Bram found himself surrendering to the inevitable.

He kissed her again and again, filling his mouth with her sweet taste. Her breathless sighs set his heart hammering. Her desperate moans made his blood burn. And when he heard his name tumble from her warm and pliant lips, it was like the sweetest music to his ears.

Because he never wanted to let her go, because in another second he would be willing to throw away everything—his location shoot, his film, his entire career—for this woman, Bram backed away. Slowly.

Dani kept her fingers curved tightly around his shoulders because she wasn't sure her watery legs would support her.

"You know, I always thought it was a cliché. But it's true, what they say," he said finally.

"What's true?" Her mouth was as dry as the arid desert ground beneath her feet. All she could manage was a ragged whisper.

He ran his knuckles up her cheek in a slow, tender sweep. "That brides are beautiful on their wedding day." Needing another taste, he leaned forward and kissed her lightly. "But you, Dani Cantrell Fortune—" he was kissing her slowly from one tingling corner of her mouth to the other "—are the most beautiful of them all." He continued his sensual quest along her jawline. Down her neck.

"You shouldn't talk to me that way," she murmured, even as she turned her head to recapture his roving lips.

"How else should a man talk to his wife?" He plucked at her parted lips, punctuating his words with brief kisses. "On their wedding night?"

"It wasn't a real wedding," she protested weakly.

Before he could respond, a man clad in a navy blue uniform appeared out of the shadows. "I'm sorry to disturb you, Mr. Fortune," the pilot said, "but we've got a report of a pretty big storm front moving in from the Pacific. If we don't take off soon, we may be forced to wait it out here on the ground."

The moment was lost. Bram felt Dani slipping away from him. "I guess you'd better go," he said.

"Yes." Dani swallowed, furiously blinking back the mutinous tears that were burning at the backs of her eyelids. She couldn't let go and cry now. Because if she did, she was afraid she'd never be able to stop.

Fighting against waves of something that felt horribly like despair, Dani decided that raging hormones must be responsible for her feeling so miserable at the idea of returning to San Francisco alone. That was all it was, she assured herself. It was all she would allow it to be.

As they stood there in the electrically charged desert night, Bram looked down into the face that had been haunting both his waking and sleeping hours for the past six weeks. He watched her valiant struggle not to weep and felt the deep tug of some foreign emotion even more elemental than his earlier desire.

During his youth, when he and Ryan and Dani had lived under the same roof, he'd found her maddening stubbornness and quicksilver temper easy to dislike. But now he realized that such personality traits were merely self-defense mechanisms designed to hide a soft and vulnerable heart.

"Have a safe flight." He bent his head and kissed her—a brief flare of heat that ended far too soon for either of them.

Although it took every ounce of willpower she possessed, Dani did not look back as she climbed the stairs and entered the cabin.

But as the plane began taxiing down the runway, she sneaked a surreptitious peek out the window and her heart took a little lurch as she saw Bram standing by the limo, both hands jammed in his pockets, watching her fly out of his life.

What she couldn't see, as the plane circled the field, rising higher and higher before finally heading west, was that he remained standing there until the bright lights of the plane had disappeared into the vast sea of stars.

TO DANI'S SURPRISE, Bram telephoned every day. The first call was to ensure that she'd gotten safely moved into his beach house. And although she assured him that everything was fine, that *she* was fine, the long-distance calls continued.

As if by mutual, unspoken consent, they stuck to safe topics: his movie, her painting, the miserable weather in the jungle, the glorious weather in Malibu. When she realized that she'd actually come to look forward to talking with Bram, Dani began to worry.

Their marriage wasn't a real one, she reminded herself firmly, as she paced the floor, watching first the minute hand, then the hour hand of the clock ticking away long past his usual nightly calling time. Hearing his voice each evening, before she went to sleep, shouldn't give her such pleasure. It shouldn't. But, heaven help her, it did.

He didn't phone that night. Or the next. At first she was worried that something terrible might have happened to him. Perhaps he'd gotten attacked by some wild jungle animal. Or been stricken with a horrible tropical disease—like malaria. Perhaps bandits had attacked the crew. Lord knows, from what she'd read of the country, it was plagued with gunrunners and jewel smugglers and drug dealers.

Why hadn't he just been satisfied with shooting here in the States, where he'd be safe? If viewers could believe Universal Studios' back lot was Cabot Cove, surely some talented set designer could have created Thailand somewhere in California?

When she tried calling the hotel where the crew was staying, only to have the long-distance operator tell her that the lines weren't working, she became absolutely frantic.

She was actually considering trying the American embassy in Bangkok until she turned on "Entertainment Tonight" and saw John Tesh reporting that Bram Fortune had been spotted carousing in the night spots on Bangkok's Patpong Road—which Tesh dutifully reported was known as the sex supermarket of Asia—with none other than Eden Vail.

An enterprising Far East wire-service reporter had faxed a photo of the couple wading barefoot through the flooded streets to the nightly entertainment program. Bram's arm was around Eden's bare waist; her brief shorts and midriff-baring halter top were wet and clung to her voluptuous body like a second skin.

So much for being eaten alive by wild animals. As for disease, Dani cattily decided that considering her alleged promiscuity, Eden Vail was undoubtedly harboring a few of the more unpleasant ones herself.

Dani was still furious when the long-awaited call finally came. Furious at Bram for having lied to her about his relationship with Eden Vail being over. Furious at herself for caring that it was not.

"Dani?" His familiar deep voice could hardly be heard over the hiss and static of the overseas line. "Can you hear me?"

"Not very well." Pride and what she had reluctantly defined as jealousy had her refusing to raise her own voice.

"Hell, I can't hear you at all," he complained. "Listen, this connection is horrendous."

She didn't answer.

"I really want to talk with you," he shouted. "Let me hang up and try again, okay?"

He took her lack of response for consent. "It's been raining cats and dogs around here, which means the phone lines are even worse than ever, so it might be a while. But I promise, I'll keep trying until I get through, okay?"

As the image of Bram and Eden in the rain flashed through her mind, Dani deliberately pressed the button, severing the long-distance connection. She placed the receiver in the desk drawer. Then she went upstairs to bed.

8

AFTER WHAT SEEMED several lifetimes, but in reality was one day more than three weeks after parting from his new bride, Bram stood in the shadows of the gallery, observing Dani with unblinking intensity.

She was dressed in a floaty creation of layers of jet silk emblazoned with gigantic scarlet poppies. The low-cut scalloped neckline skimmed her collarbone, attractively framing her face and alabaster white shoulders.

Gleaming jet hoops dangled from her ears, a trio of hammered antique-gold bracelets encircled her arms, and a gold chain dipped beneath the neckline of the dress, to nestle enticingly in the shadowed cleft between her breasts.

Her hair, as dark and shiny as a raven's wing, tumbled freely down her back, inviting a man's fingers to play in the artfully tousled waves. The memory of that wild silken mane draped across his naked thighs caused desire to pool thickly in Bram's groin.

He plucked two glasses of mineral water from the tray of a passing waiter and began wading through the crowd.

Although Dani continued to chatter merrily, laughing at some obscure joke revolving around the idea of Picasso being reduced to cranking out beer commercials for an advertising company, she was all too aware of Bram heading her way.

The small West Hollywood gallery was crammed to the rafters, yet as he approached with a long, self-assured stride, the ebullient crowd obediently made way for him. Like Moses parting the Red Sea, she thought, with a burst of irritation.

She watched as an actress, renowned for both her hot roles in a string of NC-17-rated movies, and her habit of marrying each of her costars during production, then divorcing them as soon as the picture wrapped, came up to Bram.

Although it had been a while since Madonna had made a splash wearing her underwear as outerwear at Cannes, the actress had shown up at the gallery tonight in a fifties-vintage pointy-cup bra embossed with silk fruit, a red leather micromini that barely covered the essentials, and a pair of over-the-knee red leather boots that hugged her firm thighs. In many cities the actress would have created a riot in such an outfit; here, she fit right in.

She was also obviously auditioning for Eden Vail's role in Bram's next movie and, it appeared, from the way she kept seductively licking her glossy lips, his bed. Dani watched her husband exchange a few words and a maddeningly sexy smile with the actress before moving on.

"Congratulations," Bram said, handing her one of the glasses. "Your show appears to be quite a success."

He appeared even larger than she remembered him, almost overpowering in the crowded confines of the gallery. He was wearing the same black jeans he'd worn the day she'd visited him at the studio—the day of their marriage—a black T-shirt and a well-worn black leather bomber jacket.

He obviously hadn't taken time to get a haircut in Thailand. His dark hair was shaggy, curling to his jacket collar.

"Thank you."

She accepted the glass from his outstretched hand. When their fingers touched, she felt a jolt of emotion so strong it shook her, but when she risked a cautious glance upward to see if Bram had been likewise affected, his expression gave nothing away. She took a sip of the mineral water and willed her mind and her body to calm.

"Welcome back." It was, she was discovering, difficult to remain calm, when, with a single touch, her life—her entire world—could suddenly shift on its foundations.

"It's good to be home."

Dani refrained from suggesting that if he'd foregone visiting the Bangkok night spots with Eden Vail, he might have been able to return to Los Angeles sooner.

"I've kept trying to call you, but the operator said the phone was out of order."

She shrugged her bare shoulders. "Long-distance lines are temperamental."

"Actually, she ran a check on the line and suggested the receiver might be off the hook." He was looking at her. "But you probably would have heard the signal, if that was the case."

"I expect I would," Dani agreed, refusing to admit to a thing. After all, he'd been the one in the wrong.

Another silence stretched between them.

"Quite a success," Bram repeated. He rocked back on his heels and glanced around at the white walls covered with vivid, sun-splashed landscapes and vibrant portraits surging with motion.

At first glance, the paintings seemed an energetic affirmation of the fun-filled California life-style. But a second look revealed a dark side—murky swamps of the artist's imagination brightened by unrelenting sunshine.

One painting depicted a trio of stunningly fit young women clad in minuscule bikinis, stretched out on acres of gleaming yellow sand, their oiled skin glistening a deep copper beneath the buttery rays of a benevolent sun.

On closer inspection, Bram could make out the ancient, tall-masted ship in the corner of the canvas and the marauding pirates wading through the surf, cutlasses raised, intent on attacking the blissfully oblivious sunbathers.

Another canvas showed a couple making passionate love atop a seaside cliff. As their tortured, ecstatic faces revealed them to be at the moment of orgasm, a jagged lightning bolt emerged from a single puffy white cloud overhead to strike them.

A rowboat drifted on the placid waters of an inland lake lined with weeping willows. In the boat, a woman, dressed in a white Edwardian dress and holding a parasol, was lying in the embrace of a man dressed in a white suit and straw hat. Enjoying the peaceful day, both lovers remained blissfully unaware of the shark swimming behind the boat.

As unsettling as Dani's works were, several of the canvases bore small red stickers in the bottom right-hand corner.

"Looks as if you're going to sell out," Bram commented. "You must be feeling on top of the world right now."

"It's always nice to have my work appreciated."

His brazen bedroom eyes moved over her face with the impact of a caress. "I'd heard you were talented." They settled on her lips, stealing her breath away. "Even so, I'll admit to being impressed."

When he reached out and twined a lock of Dani's unruly hair around his finger, she stiffened. For the first time in a very long while, Dani felt horribly vulnerable.

It was a casual touch, unplanned, designed to please himself. But as he watched, the color suddenly fled Dani's face.

Secrets. They were lurking behind those beautiful, dark eyes. If he hadn't known better, Bram would have thought Dani was actually afraid of him.

That, of course, was impossible. But something had just happened. Something Bram had every intention of getting to the bottom of.

"Let's get out of this zoo," he suggested.

His hand had just cupped her elbow possessively, when an ebullient man, clad in a gold silk duster over black linen slacks and a black silk shirt, came up to her.

"Dani, darling," he gushed, air-kissing both her cheeks. "Congratulations on an absolute tour de force." He had a beard clipped in a Vandyke style and his dark hair had been pulled back into a ponytail, all the better to display high, slanted cheekbones any cover girl would have killed for.

"These latest paintings are your best work yet," the man's companion, clad in a flowing white poet's shirt, white scarf knotted aviator-style about the throat and brown leather pants, immediately agreed. His gleaming black hair was fashioned in Rastafarian braids. "In fact, I adore the Olivia Street painting so much that I bought it for myself." He turned to Bram. His lips, surrounded by a sooty beard, curved in a friendly smile. "I'm very aesthetically aware," he revealed. "I have a deep, visceral need to be surrounded by beautiful things."

Bram nodded. "I feel the same way." He slanted a seductive glance Dani's way, which suggested exactly what "beautiful thing" he'd like to have surrounding him right now.

The men's interested gazes went from Bram to Dani— who'd recovered enough to glare daggers at her new husband—then back to Bram.

"I'm Arturo Rodriguez," the first man introduced himself. "Proprietor of this gallery and discoverer of new and hot artists such as our darling Dani." He extended his hand. Diamonds flashed on his fingers, gold gleamed at his wrist.

Bram shook the gallery owner's hand. "Bram Fortune."

"Ah, the wunderkind." Dollar signs began to gleam in Arturo's brown eyes. "And our darling Dani's recent patron."

When she'd relocated from San Francisco, Dani had had no choice but to tell Arturo that she'd moved into Bram's house. What she hadn't told him was the circumstances behind the move.

After seeing the news-wire photo of her husband and his lover on television, Dani had come to the conclusion that their arrangement would never work.

Besides, even if he wasn't still involved with Eden Vail, the way he'd rushed her off to Las Vegas, without even giving her time to think, was proof that Bram Fortune was every bit as controlling as Peter Bannister. That being the case, for all her self-congratulations about putting the past behind her and getting on with her life, despite all her clever rationalizations, the unpleasant truth was that by marrying Bram she'd leapt from the frying pan into the flames.

Living under the same roof with this man, even for the duration of her pregnancy, would be like playing with fire. Not only did she have a feeling Bram could make things very hot indeed, Dani knew that if she didn't back away now, she would get badly burned.

Which was why she'd decided that they should cut their losses and call it quits before the baby was born.

Since news of their marriage had miraculously not yet leaked out, Dani had chosen not to correct Arturo's understandable assumption that she was the director's latest mistress.

Now, about to be caught in her lie of omission, Dani fatalistically waited for the truth to come out.

"I was sorry to hear of your recent loss," Arturo offered.

"A tragedy," his companion murmured.

"Thank you." The death of his brother still pained. Bram figured it probably always would.

"Are you a collector?" Arturo asked.

"I've bought a painting or two." Bram put his arm around Dani's waist. Ignoring the way she went as rigid as a spear, he rested his hand on her hip in a possessive gesture. "But I'm here tonight in my role as supportive husband."

"Husband?"

The gallery owner's confusion was obvious. His gaze dropped to Dani's left hand, which Bram had noticed was currently unadorned.

"Dani, dear heart, you've been keeping secrets," Arturo's companion complained.

"It's a long story."

Dani was furious at Bram for making their relationship public this way. Although they might be fairly new in town, Arturo and his longtime companion, Dennis Laughton, already had a wide circle of friends and acquaintances. And, as much as she cared for Arturo—and knew he cared for her—he was incapable of keeping a secret.

She glared up at Bram, only to find herself trapped in the depths of the intense eyes looking back at her. They stood there, inches apart, oblivious to the crowd swirling around them and the two bearded men watching with undisguised interest.

They could have been the only two people in the room; the buzz of conversation seemed to fade into the distance until the only sound was the *swoosh-swoosh-swoosh* of the overhead ceiling fan, relentlessly churning the air, blending the heady scents of designer perfumes into a suffocating cloud.

"Dani can fill you in on all the details some other time," Bram said, his eyes locked with hers. "We were just about to leave." His fingers tightened on her elbow. "Come along, dear. It's getting late." He bent down and whispered in her ear. "And you need your rest."

Dani shook off his proprietory touch. "In case you haven't noticed, Bram, I happen to be working." Her tone was icy, her eyes were an intriguing combination of frost and fire that Bram had never before witnessed at the same time in any other woman.

Appearing unperturbed by Dani's rising irritation, he ran one hand down her hair in a soothing, husbandly gesture.

The other settled again at her hip. "I always notice everything about you, sweetheart."

He glanced over at the gallery owner. "I hope you won't mind me stealing your artist away."

"Of course not," Arturo said with an accommodating smile.

Irritated by the way her friend seemed to have joined the enemy camp, Dani plucked Bram's hand away.

"I think I should stay," she insisted, holding herself rigid, even as the idly caressing fingers were creating a disturbing warmth. "In case a prospective buyer has any questions."

"Oh, I think you've mingled enough for one evening, Dani," Arturo interjected quickly. He ignored her scowl. "So long as the food and drink hold up, I'm sure no one will even miss you."

"You're so good for my ego, Arturo," Dani muttered dryly. "But I'll leave when I'm good and ready. And I'm not ready."

Rather than seeming annoyed by her refusal, Bram remained disturbingly patient. Indeed, as he stood there, almost looming over her, Dani had the uneasy impression that he was willing to wait all night, if that's what it took.

It crossed her mind that despite the sophisticated Hollywood world he lived and worked in, Bramwell Fortune was definitely a predator. Dani decided that were she to paint him, she'd portray him as a pirate. Or some ancient warrior, clad in a loincloth and armed with only a spear and that dangerous, unwavering patience.

"Don't tell me you're afraid to be alone with your own husband," he said finally.

His smooth taunt hit a little too close to home. Dani would rather go skinny-dipping off Zuma Beach with sharks than admit to the vague warnings that had been whispering up her nerve ends from the moment he'd walked into the gallery. Warnings that were growing stronger by the moment.

"Afraid? Of you?" She raised her chin, hating herself for finding that dark blue gaze so hypnotic. And, dammit, exciting. "Don't be ridiculous."

She tossed her head, causing a cloud of dark hair to drift over her eye. Before she could shake it out of the way, Bram reached out and brushed it off her cheek.

The seemingly casual gesture was too intimate for comfort. Dani's mouth went dry. Nerves stretched painfully tight, she backed away.

She'd tensed as if she'd expected him to hit her. What the hell kind of man did she think he was? Bram would be the first to admit that he'd never been the Boy Scout Ryan had been. But neither had he ever—under any circumstances—considered lifting a hand to a woman. The idea that Dani might think otherwise was like a wasp sting to his ego.

Bram turned to Arturo, who was no longer even attempting to conceal his delight with this unexpected drama. "Before I leave, I want to buy one of Dani's paintings for myself."

"You don't have to—"

"Which one?" Arturo asked, quickly cutting off Dani's protest. "Oh, I do hope it's not the montage of Rose Bowl queens about to be attacked by land sharks."

"Sanji Yakomoto's been staring covetously at that one for the past hour," Dennis revealed conspiratorially. "He tried telling Arturo that it was a bit pricey for his budget, but we figure he'll cave in at any moment."

"Actually," Bram divulged, "the one I had in mind is the portrait of the young woman standing on the cliff overlooking the sea."

Like the rest of Dani's works, the painting was one of unsettling cheerfulness laced with a sly, deadly ambiguity. The woman depicted in the painting was dressed all in white and carried a sunshine yellow basket overflowing with brightly hued flowers. Behind her, an enormous gray stone house loomed darkly in the mists; filmy figures that could have been lost souls, or perhaps, merely wisps of smoke, rose skyward from its many chimneys.

The painting had been the first she'd painted after the beating. It was so painfully autobiographical that she hadn't wanted anyone to ever see it.

Unfortunately, Arturo had discovered the painting hidden behind a stack of blank canvases and had insisted, against Dani's protests, on including it in the show. "Why on earth would you want that one?" she asked in a frail voice that reminded Bram of how she'd sounded when she'd first learned that Ryan was dead.

"I figure the way you're selling out, it'll be a good investment," Bram said obliquely. He didn't add that for some reason, the young woman on the cliff reminded him of Dani.

"I don't want that in our home," she insisted, conveniently forgetting that she'd decided to move out of the Malibu house as soon as Bram returned from Thailand.

"Fine." She looked fragile enough to crumble. More secrets, Bram thought. More layers. Why had he ever considered this woman uncomplicated?

"I'll keep it at my office." He handed Arturo a gray embossed business card. "Please have it delivered to my offices at Eclipse Studios. I'll send a check tomorrow."

"Oh, take your time," the gallery owner insisted expansively. "Your credit is always good with us, Mr. Fortune." He kissed Dani on the cheek. "Best wishes, little one."

"Good luck," Dennis chimed in, kissing her in turn.

She was going to need more than luck to get her through tonight, Dani knew. If his maddeningly possessive behavior thus far this evening was any indication, Bram was not going to turn cartwheels over her request for an immediate annulment.

Her mind was whirling, considering and discarding numerous tactics as she accompanied Bram through the crowd.

They were almost to the door when Peter Bannister moved deftly in front of them.

9

"HELLO, DANI."

She stiffened. "Hello, Peter. This is a surprise." Her tight voice suggested that it was not a pleasant one.

"I read about your opening in last Sunday's *Times*. I hope you don't mind my coming."

Dani shrugged with a nonchalance she was a very long way from feeling. It had been bad enough having him stalk her in San Francisco. To think that he'd followed her here was chilling.

"It's a free world."

His pale blue eyes, veiled ever so slightly by the lenses of dark-framed glasses, narrowed. "Gracious as always, aren't you?"

"Didn't anyone ever tell you that's no way to talk to a lady?" Bram interjected. His voice was low and dangerous.

"Please, Bram." Dani put her left hand on her husband's arm and felt the dangerous tension of steely muscle beneath the supple leather. "I can handle this." She'd already allowed one Fortune brother to fight her battles with this man for her. Stronger now, Dani wanted—needed—to prove to Peter Bannister once and for all that she was capable of standing up to him on her own.

Bram had felt her tension. Her momentary fear. And now, looking down into her face, he saw her resolve.

"Whatever you say, sweetheart."

His arm tightened slightly around her waist, pulling her against him. Although he didn't like standing impotently by, he'd let her take care of the situation. But he also wanted the guy, whoever he was, to understand that Dani was not alone.

"But don't take too long." He dropped a brief, husbandly kiss atop her head. "After three long lonely weeks apart, we've got a lot of catching up to do."

"I wouldn't want to keep you," Peter said. His voice was silky smooth, his smile warm, belying the ice in his gaze. "I just wanted to congratulate you, Dani. You look absolutely beautiful. As always." Myriad sharp remarks danced on the tip of her tongue. She thought of all the ugly, body-concealing clothes he'd made her wear during their marriage. Remembered the hateful accusations he'd thrown at her as he'd ripped them off.

Deciding he wasn't worth the effort it took to throw all those past sins back in his deceptively handsome face, Dani merely said, "Thank you."

"Aren't you going to introduce me to your friend?" he asked, acknowledging Bram for the first time.

"Bram Fortune, Peter Bannister," Dani obliged flatly. She decided it was definite progress that she could say Peter's name without choking.

So this guy in the custom-tailored tux was the man who'd stolen Dani from Ryan so many years ago. Obviously, Bram mused, Dani had been struck by a severe case of temporary insanity during her time in France.

"Nice to meet you," Peter said. "I've admired your work."

"Thanks."

Loyalty to his brother, along with the vibrations he was picking up from Dani, kept Bram from accepting the outstretched hand.

"I was hoping you'd join me for a late supper, Dani," Peter suggested with a winning smile as he lowered his hand to his side again. Only someone carefully watching his eyes, as Bram was, would have detected the anger the intentional slight had stirred. "To celebrate your success. And drink to old times together."

This time it was Bram who stiffened. "It's supposed to be a party, Peter," Dani said. "Not a wake." She flashed him her sweetest, falsest smile. "But do enjoy the evening."

Linking her arm in Bram's, Dani turned to leave. Although she remained outwardly calm, her knees were trembling.

There was a sudden crack, like a small-caliber pistol shot, as the plastic champagne glass shattered in Peter Bannister's hand.

Enraged at being so summarily dismissed, he reached out, grabbed Dani's bare arm and spun her back toward him. "I want to talk to you, dammit."

The sight of another man's hand on Dani caused Bram to see red. He made a low snarl deep in his throat, like the warning growl of a timber wolf.

"If you want to remain alive," he said in a deceptively soft voice, "I'd suggest you take your hand off my wife."

"Wife?" Peter's gaze raked over Dani in a scornful way that had once possessed the ability to make her blood run cold with fear. But no longer! she realized with a sudden thrill. "You actually married this slut?"

"That's it." He grabbed Bannister and turned him in the direction of the door. "You're out of here," he growled. "Before I decide to mess up that pretty-boy face."

Stupidly, Dani's former husband swung his right fist at Bram, who countered with a short jab that connected with Bannister's nose. A follow-up powerful left cross slammed into his jaw and sent him flying.

As Peter Bannister landed on a silver tray of golden crab puffs and mesquite-grilled artichoke hearts with a force that caused the table legs to collapse, Dani cried out and flash-bulbs exploded.

"Bram, please!" Although Dani couldn't deny that she'd received some satisfaction in watching her former tormentor receive a bit of his own painful medicine, she was terrified that Bram might follow through on the murder she could see in his eyes. "He's not worth this."

If it hadn't been for a reluctance to further disrupt Dani's show, Bram would cheerfully have killed the son of a bitch. And even that might not have restrained him if Dani's ex had made even the slightest move to defend himself.

Instead, Peter stayed on the floor, fumbling around for his glasses, which had landed somewhere amid the scattered canapés.

"You broke my nose, dammit!" He dabbed with a snowy handkerchief at the crimson blood that was pouring from his nostrils.

"Consider yourself lucky this time," Bram retorted, his eyes fierce and deadly. "There are approximately two-hundred-and-six bones in the human body, Bannister. Lay one hand on this woman ever again, and I promise, I'll break them all. Slowly. One at a time."

Peter Bannister might be down, but he was yet to be counted out. Finally locating his glasses, he shoved them back onto his face. One of the lenses had shattered into a spider-web network of cracks. "I should have you arrested for assault and battery."

"Go right ahead and try." Bram leaned down and yanked him from the floor.

Out of the corner of his eye, Bram saw a pair of grim-faced individuals, obviously plainclothes security guards, wading through the crowd. The buzz of excited conversation filled the room like the sound of a thousand angry bees.

"You'll regret this, Fortune."

"No." Bram jerked Bannister's arm behind his back. "But you will. If you come anywhere near my wife again." He shoved him toward the guards. "Get this bastard out of here," he ordered. "Before he ruins a lovely evening by causing a commotion."

"Yes, sir," the guards replied in unison.

As upset as she was by what had just happened, Dani couldn't help noticing the way both men immediately accepted Bram as the individual in charge.

"You'll pay for this, Fortune," Peter shouted back over his shoulder as the guards took him away. "You'll both pay!"

Ignoring the threats, Bram turned toward Dani. "Ready to go home, sweetheart?" His voice was amazingly calm, considering what had just transpired. But as he held out his hand to her, Dani could see a remnant of icy rage lingering in his eyes.

They were, unsurprisingly, the center of attention. A hush had fallen over the gallery. It was suddenly so quiet, you could hear a pin—or, Dani considered with a surprising burst of dark humor, an ex-husband—drop.

"An excellent idea," she agreed.

Dani turned on Bram as soon as they were outside. "I am absolutely furious at you, Bramwell Fortune!"

"At me?" He stopped dead in his tracks and stared down at her. "*You're* furious at *me?*" he repeated.

Robertson Boulevard—where gay dance clubs shared space with health clubs, galleries and trendy beauty salons—was the scene of endless activity, as patrons of the cafés and bars spilled out onto the sidewalk. The flow of pedestrians surged around Dani and Bram as they stood there, toe to toe.

She dragged a hand through her hair, pushing it away from her face. "You caused a scene."

"Excuse me," he countered sarcastically. "He called you a—" Bram couldn't say the unsavory word. Not when referring to this woman. "He insulted you. And he touched you."

"*Touched*," she emphasized, refusing to admit, even to herself, the familiar fear that had skimmed up her spine when she'd felt those treacherous fingers curl around her wrist. "I'm more than capable of handling myself, Bram."

"He frightened you, dammit."

She couldn't deny it. "That's not the point. I had things under control. And besides, I don't recall appointing you to be my white knight."

"Of course you did."

"When?"

"When you married me."

Although their sham marriage was precisely what she wanted to discuss, Dani had the good sense to realize that this was neither the time nor the place.

"We both know the reason I married you," she reminded him. "And it wasn't to hire on a protector."

He shook his head. "If you're suggesting that I should stand by and let some creep insult, then manhandle my wife, you may as well save your breath, Dani. Because it isn't going to happen. Not in this lifetime."

"You ruined my show!"

"Hell, instead of yelling at me, you should be thanking me for livening things up. In case you hadn't noticed, sweetheart, a lull was beginning to set in."

"I guess I was too busy watching Arturo fawn over my husband to notice much of anything else," Dani retorted. "Lord," she said as a thought occurred to her, "you can't say Arturo's L.A. career didn't start out with a bang! I hope he's not too angry with us."

Bram decided he liked the idea that she'd referred to them as a team. Like Butch Cassidy and the Sundance Kid. Or Bonnie and Clyde.

"Actually, we undoubtedly set the standard. He'll have a hard time topping our entertainment value at his next show."

Bram flexed his fingers, remembering the satisfying feel of cartilage breaking beneath his fist. He hadn't been in a fight since his freshman year at Tahoe City's Evergreen High School.

Then again, Bram considered, he hadn't run across anything—or anyone—worth fighting for. Until Dani.

"Besides, your ex started it," he reminded her, wondering if Dani had any idea how much control it had taken not to beat the bastard to a bloody pulp. "I can't see you married to him."

She managed a laugh. "Neither can I. Now."

Whatever had happened between the pair, Bram suspected that it was proof of Dani's inner strength that she'd survived what he was beginning to suspect must have been a brutal marriage.

Bram wondered idly if Ryan had known the particulars of Dani's relationship with Bannister, then decided that he undoubtedly had. That explained his steadfast unwillingness to discuss his fiancée's former marriage. It also explained the uncharacteristic fury that had burned in his brother's eyes the one time Bram had idly questioned him about it.

"Let's go get something to eat," he said, opting to change the subject. "I'm starving." Having driven to the gallery immediately after his flight had landed at LAX, he'd foregone dinner in order to see Dani again.

He took her elbow and guided her around a crowd of teenagers, their spiked hair dyed every color of the rainbow. Clad in black jeans and black turtleneck T-shirts, they were unrelentingly androgynous.

"Actually, I thought I'd send out for an anchovy pizza."

Although he'd had something French and dimly lit in mind, on second thought, Bram decided that after three weeks of eating God-knows-what kind of mystery food in the jungle, the idea of a pizza and a cold beer sounded like nirvana. But anchovies?

"Is this one of those pregnant-lady cravings I've read about?" he asked as he led her to a British-racing-green Jaguar parked at the curb.

"I think so," she admitted.

"Then we'd better indulge it," Bram concluded. "But we're only ordering anchovies on your side."

She laughed, feeling strangely, incredibly lighthearted. "You've got yourself a deal."

As Bram entered his beachfront home, it crossed his mind that it was at the same time both familiar and different.

"You've moved the furniture around."

"Just a little." Dani felt suddenly defensive about what at the time had seemed an inspired idea. "All I did was turn the couch away from the television and toward the window, so I could enjoy the sunsets, but if you'd rather have it back the other way—"

"No." He realized he'd unwittingly made her nervous and regretted having said anything. "It's perfect." After all, an evening spent watching ESPN couldn't begin to compare with lying on the sofa with his new bride in his arms, watching the sun sink into the Pacific.

He glanced around, taking in the cheery bouquet of tulips in bright primary colors that added color to the stark white interior. A Waterford bowl had been filled with delicate pink and ivory seashells. A needlepoint pillow depicting a trio of sailboats on a sparkling blue sea adorned a corner of the alabaster white leather sofa.

Always before, when he returned from location, Bram came home to an empty house. Having never associated living alone with "lonely," that had never bothered him. Until tonight, when he walked into a house filled with Dani's presence.

"This is your house now, Dani," he reminded her. "You're free to do anything you want. Including gutting the place and starting from scratch."

"Oh, I wouldn't want to do that," Dani said quickly. Although there were a few changes she'd like to make. If she were going to be living here forever. Which, she reminded herself firmly, she wasn't.

Bram saw a faint shadow move across her eyes. "The only reason I said anything at all was because I was concerned about you moving furniture," he explained. "In your condition."

"Oh." Her brow cleared. "You don't have to worry. Arturo and Dennis did all the heavy lifting."

"Remind me to thank them. If they're still talking to me tomorrow."

"Oh, don't worry. They'll undoubtedly be charming," Dani assured him. "At least until your check clears."

The laughter came dancing back into her eyes. Bram stood there, drinking in the sight of her, momentarily transfixed.

"You are so lovely." His voice was oddly distant, as if he were talking more to himself than to her. "You quite literally take my breath away."

Talk about taking the breath away! Enmeshed in the silken snare of his intimate gaze, Dani was having trouble drawing air into her lungs. She pressed her hand against her breast, as if to ensure that her heart was still beating.

The way he kept looking at her stirred emotions that were better left safely banked. Warm, muddled, aching feelings that threatened to confuse even further a relationship that had already been sorely complicated by her unplanned pregnancy.

By marrying Bram so quickly, she had dived into dangerous, uncharted waters. The only wise course of action—Dani reminded herself of her earlier resolve—was to end this sham of a marriage before she found herself in over her head.

"The dress is new." Her nerveless fingers plucked at the bright skirt. She decided against revealing she'd been forced to go shopping this afternoon when she discovered she couldn't zip the gown she'd planned to wear.

"The dress is lovely." The way he was looking at her gave Dani the impression he could see right through the flowered silk. "But I have a feeling it's the body beneath the dress that's making me hot." He ran his hand across her bare shoulder-blades with a casual possessiveness that made her ache. His fingers toyed with the slender gold chain around her neck. "Let's go upstairs and take it off so we can see whether it's the lady or the dress."

The lady or the tiger, Bram thought. Three months ago he'd opened the door to his cabin and discovered both waiting for him.

He'd fully expected to forget Dani as soon as he returned to Los Angeles. After Ryan's funeral when she'd infuriatingly stayed in his mind, tormenting him with erotic memories, he'd tried telling himself that the chemistry between them had been an aberration. An understandable attempt at sexual healing.

But since then, most particularly when he'd found himself missing her the entire time he'd been in Thailand, Bram had come to realize that something had happened that stolen night with Dani in the cabin.

"Bram." His name was little more than a soft shadow of sound. "You promised."

"I promised not to do anything you didn't want to do," he reminded her.

Dear Lord, that was precisely the problem! What Dani wanted Bram to do and what some heretofore-unheard-from, horribly logical voice in her mind told her she should allow him to do, were two entirely different things.

"I'd better call for that pizza."

She could deny it until hell froze over, but she wanted him, dammit. Every bit as much as he wanted her. Bram could see it in her remarkable eyes.

He debated telling Dani that the pizza could wait until they'd satisfied a more elemental hunger that had been building for weeks. Then, as if on cue, his stomach growled, reminding him all too vividly that man did not live by love alone.

"Don't forget," he said as he left the living room, and headed up the stairs to take a shower. He felt grungy after the long transpacific flight. "Anchovies on your side only."

Bram was not encouraged by the fact that Dani had obviously foregone the master suite and moved into the guest bedroom.

He was encouraged by the evidence that she had apparently not been able to resist the lure of the most hedonistic room in the house. A row of colored bottles filled with crystal bath salts lined the tiled edge of the oversize sunken Jacuzzi bathtub. A pink bar of perfumed soap that hadn't been in the four-headed shower when he'd left for Thailand smelled like her. As did the navy blue towel hanging on the rack.

A brush—the silver-backed, antique kind he often saw in jewelry stores but had never realized women actually used—rested on the white marble countertop. A few long strands of jet hair had tangled in the bristles. An aqua jar claimed space beside the brush.

After emerging from the shower, Bram idly unscrewed the lid of the jar, dipped a finger into the fragrant pink cream and lifted it to his nose. As he inhaled Dani's familiar scent, desire slammed into him.

Memories of that scent had tortured him every steamy night in the jungle, causing him to toss and turn amid sweat-drenched sheets, his fevered mind filled with images of Dani, his body aching with unrequited, painful need.

There had been, as always on a movie set, attractive, available women, including his female star who'd assured him that he would be more than welcome in her bed. But things had changed since that night with Dani. He had changed.

The rock lyrics had it wrong, Bram determined, as he put the lid back on the jar. If he couldn't be with the one he loved, it was no longer enough to love the one he was with.

Love. The word shocked him out of his sensual reverie. Was it possible? Bram wondered. He wanted Dani. He was, after all, a very physical man and she was an incredibly desirable woman. He'd make no excuse for the lure of hormones.

But it was obviously more than desire that had kept him celibate those long and lonely weeks in Thailand. It was more than mere sexual need that had him missing her like crazy.

He'd thought of her too much. Too exclusively. During those long frustrating days when he should have been concentrating on his work, she didn't just enter his mind, she invaded it.

Of course, he cared for Dani. She was, after all, the mother of his child—unplanned or not—and he'd been brought up to value family. She was also, for better or worse, his wife. And, although their marriage may have started out as a match of convenience, Bram was vaguely surprised by how seriously he was taking his wedding vows.

He had never given a great deal of thought to the idea of marriage. Unlike Ryan, who'd probably decided to marry Dani while they were both still in the cradle, Bram had always been quite content with his bachelor status.

He'd enjoyed being free, with no ties, no strings. His career encouraged him to be selfish; his work was both demanding and fulfilling.

And, needless to say, there were always willing, available women to fill in the gaps. Women who understood the rules of the game they were playing. Women who had no more desire to get entangled in an emotional relationship than he did.

So who would have suspected that a single act of forbidden passion on what had been the most painful night of his life, could end up turning his life—his entire world—upside down?

He didn't love her. He couldn't love her. Although he had no firsthand knowledge of the emotion that poets and songwriters waxed so lyrical about, he refused to believe that love could come this quickly. This easily.

But, God, how he wanted her! The need that had been building for weeks, was twisting his gut, eating away at his insides.

All his life, he'd done exactly what he'd wanted to do.

Gotten what he'd wanted.

And although he'd tried to tell himself that this outrageous attraction for his brother's fiancée would pass, what he wanted, more with each passing day, was Dani Cantrell. Dani Fortune, he corrected.

Impatient with his train of thought—which invariably involved Dani lying naked and hot beneath him—Bram dressed quickly, in jeans and a loose-weave cream sweater, not bothering to dry his hair.

He jammed his bare feet into a pair of ancient sneakers and then, her scent still teasing his nostrils, finger combed the thick mane of shaggy black hair back from his forehead.

Then he went downstairs to join his bride.

10

BACK IN THE LIVING ROOM, the spicy, enticing scent of pot-pourri emanating from a flowered porcelain dish Dani had placed on the granite-slab coffee table mingled with the fragrance of the tulips and a faint odor of turpentine.

The pizza, loaded with double cheese, was thick and gooey, the beer cold, the company perfect.

From the way she made her half of the pizza disappear, Bram was pleased to see that Dani's morning sickness must have abated.

"That was great," he said after they'd finished eating. They were sitting at the table she'd moved from the formal, sel-dom-used dining room into the living room, again, she'd explained, to take advantage of the ocean view.

"I imagine you're accustomed to more sophisticated fare." She kicked herself for not having planned a more advantageous setting for this all-important discussion.

He laughed at that. A deep, hearty sound that Dani found herself liking far too much for comfort. "Are you suggesting that I'd rather order out from Spago than Pizza Hut?"

"Well, you are the one who mentioned the ridiculously expensive goat-cheese pizza," she reminded. "The day of the funeral," she elaborated, at Bram's blank look.

"Oh, that." The memory threatened to put a pall over the reunion Bram had been looking forward to for weeks. He shrugged. "Just because I sometimes eat at what the rest of the world considers a trendy Hollywood hot spot doesn't mean that I can't still enjoy the basics of life.

"Like buttered popcorn at the movies, a dodger dog slathered with yellow mustard at the ballpark—"

"Peanuts at the circus," Dani supplied.

"Exactly." He grinned his approval. "And when I really feel like slumming, I order a take-out pizza with double cheese."

He tipped the long-necked bottle back and took another drink of dark beer. "You know," he said, changing the subject, "I really am impressed with your success. That's quite a coup. Having a one-woman exhibit."

His admiration seemed genuine. His smile was warm and unthreatening. During the casual take-out supper, Dani had begun to relax. Almost.

"It was nice," she agreed. "Usually, showing with other artists, I have to try and fit my work into some theme." She gave him a genuine smile of her own. "It was wonderful being allowed to take chances."

"It's always satisfying, being able to express yourself freely," Bram agreed.

"Oh, my art isn't about expressing myself," Dani quickly corrected. "It's about reflecting society."

Bram frowned as he considered that idea in light of the paintings he'd seen. "Funny. I wouldn't have guessed you to have such a paranoid view of the world." Having met her husband, however, Bram decided that perhaps he could understand the theme of unexpected horror that ran through her work.

Dani shrugged, wondering how they'd gotten on to the subject of her intimate feelings. "I don't. Not really."

All right, so it wasn't exactly the entire truth. Peter had altered her outlook on life. She was neither as naive nor as trusting as she'd been before her marriage.

She took a drink of ice tea, hoping it would calm her nerves. It didn't. "Is that how you saw my work? As an exercise in paranoia?"

"Not exactly paranoia," he decided after a moment's consideration. "At first, your use of bold colors seems to evoke dazzling optimism. But after a closer look, your paintings are darker and more complicated than they appear on the surface. In that respect, I'd say they're a bit like the artist herself."

Dani had already come to realize that Bram was not a man to accept things—or people—at first glance. That idea led to a second, more unpalatable thought that his ability to recognize her inner shadows made him even more dangerous.

If he could read her mind, if he could sense all her feelings, would he realize that she was beginning to care for him far more than she should?

"My art is very personal," she allowed. She lowered her gaze in an attempt to hide her thoughts.

"That's probably as it should be." He polished off the beer. "I feel the same way about my own work."

"Ah, yes." Relieved to have the spotlight taken off her, Dani leaned back and crossed her legs. "How did the last days of shooting go?"

"Despite the fact that the monsoons forced us to stop the shoot a day early, we ended up getting some good stuff. It's going to take some heavy editing, but it should work out."

"I'm glad." Despite her vow to herself not to dignify his ongoing affair with Eden Vail, Dani couldn't help but ask, "I guess, since you couldn't shoot every day, you managed to make a little time for some sight-seeing."

"Actually, we were too busy moving from one flooded hotel to another. A little rain and the entire damn country turns into one big lake."

Her mood darkened as she thought about the photo of a barefoot Bram and Eden wading through the water-filled streets of Bangkok's notorious red-light district. But, what had she expected? Neither she nor Bram had married for love. What right did she have to be jealous?

A little silence settled over them. When he stretched his long legs out beneath the table and brushed hers, Dani felt a tingle of something indiscernible race through her veins. Pleasure? Desire? Fear? Even a bit of all three?

Her lovely face was an open book. Bram watched the emotions wash over Dani's features in waves. When he viewed what could only be described as fear, he wondered what the hell he'd done to make her afraid of him. Didn't she realize that he had nothing in common with Bannister?

"Why don't we move this conversation to the couch?" he suggested. His eyes flicked to her mouth, lingering there as if he were imagining the taste of her lips before returning to her still-wary gaze.

The idea of watching the moon-gilded waters wash up onto the beach while lying in Bram's strong arms sounded tempting and terrifying at the same time. It wasn't that she was afraid of him. Certainly not in the way she'd been afraid of Peter.

What Dani feared was what Bram could come to mean to her.

"I should probably throw away the pizza box," she said, stalling.

"I'll do it later." He smiled across the table. "Isn't it a husband's duty to take out the trash?"

"I don't know." When she'd lived in Peter's house there'd been a host of stiffly polite servants to take care of the day-to-day chores. Indeed, by the second week, Dani had given up even trying to sneak into the kitchen to make a peanut-butter sandwich for herself.

"No matter," he said with forced casualness. He stood and held his hand out to her. "We can make up our domestic rules as we go along."

He made it sound so simple, Dani thought. So real.

"Please come sit with me, Dani." It was the closest he'd ever come to begging in his life. "I've missed you."

She was twisting the paper napkin in her hands. "I missed you, too," she whispered. While the response might not be the prudent one, under the circumstances, Dani knew there was no way she could lie. Not about something so elemental.

Bram knew the halted admission had cost her.

He also knew he'd waited long enough to make love to his wife.

"Dani." He came around the table, watching awareness flood into her eyes. No longer relaxed, she looked poised for flight.

"Don't," she said, as he plucked the shredded napkin from her fingers and tossed it into the empty pizza box.

"You're my wife." He took hold of her hands and coaxed her to her feet. "I'm your husband."

"In name only."

As she felt her hands being swallowed up in his, Dani remembered all too well how those same hands had felt on her body—soothing and arousing all at the same time.

That thought led to another, of how those fists had so easily dispensed with Peter. Bram was strong. And hard. And even as he had made her feel safe and protected, he also made her feel soft.

Dani didn't want to feel soft. It wasn't safe to be soft. She had the scars—both physical and emotional—to prove that softness made a woman weak. And vulnerable. Something she'd vowed never to be again.

Bram watched her eyes go from soft to blank, and cursed inwardly. "You can't deny that you haven't been remembering what it felt like." He lifted her frigid hands and touched his lips to her knuckles. "And wondering if it will be that way again."

"We don't even know each other." She struggled, cleared the lump from her throat and tried again. "Not really."

"I know that your pulse leaps when I do this." He turned her hand and kissed the inside of her wrist.

This wasn't smart, Dani told herself. Not smart at all.

"And this." His lips feathered irresistible heat in the crook of her elbow. Dani could feel the sparks racing all the way to her fingertips.

"Bram . . ."

He ignored her faint protest and continued his sensual assault. "And this." His treacherous lips moved to her neck, creating havoc with every atom in her body. "I know I can make you tremble when I touch you." He pressed his palm against her breast, and was rewarded by the wild, out-of-control beat of her heart.

His touch was like flame, branding her through the silk of her dress. "It's just nerves," she said, even as she arched against his hand, mutely encouraging him to continue.

He tugged her long jet earring off with his teeth. "Do I make you nervous?"

The pleasure was almost too much to bear. Dani closed her eyes. "No," she lied on a soft, ragged moan.

"Perhaps it's leftover tension from your show." He slid his knee between her legs.

"Perhaps." Dani decided not to admit that these weakening feelings were due to something a great deal more elemental than her gallery opening. "Or, I suppose it could be the full moon."

"The full moon was last week."

"The waning moon, then." He pressed his thigh wickedly against her. "Or the tides."

When she felt herself beginning to sway helplessly in his arms, Dani forced her eyes open and stiffened both her spine and her resolve.

"After all, it's a well-known biological fact that seventy percent of the human body is made up of water, the very same percentage of water that makes up the earth's surface.

How can we help but be affected by things like moons and tides?"

Her eyes were too bright. Her voice too brittle. "Dani," Bram soothed expertly as his hands skimmed down the sides of her body, from her shoulders to her hips, "we both know that what we're feeling right now doesn't have anything to do with moons or tides or any other fanciful notion."

His leg was rubbing against her, slowly, enticingly. As she began to move as well, Dani heard Bram's raw murmur of approval.

His fingers crushed her skirt, raising the hem to grant his hands access to flesh he recalled being every bit as soft as the silk covering it.

"We really need to talk," Dani managed on a gasp.

"We can talk later." He cupped her feminine heat and found her as hot and damp as his most erotic fantasy.

It was happening again. Another minute of Bram's seductive, sensual torment and Dani knew the last remnants of her control would crumble, like a sand castle at high tide.

"I want to talk now."

Bram was hot and frustrated and his body throbbed. He knew that he could change her mind. That he could toss her down on the nearby couch and before she could tell him one more time how much she didn't want to make love, she'd be begging him to take her.

But such sexual conquest, while easing the ache in his groin, would do nothing to prove to her that he wasn't the brute her first husband had obviously been.

As he watched moisture well up in her remarkable eyes, Bram realized belatedly that Dani was frightened. Frightened of him, of his strength, perhaps even of her own ungovernable passions. To take her now, even with her consent, while her emotions were so tattered, would not only be wrong, it would be unconscionable.

"Whatever you want." His voice, as he readjusted her clothing, was rough. "So," he said on a long, frustrated sigh, "what do you want to talk about?"

"Actually, I've spent a great deal of time thinking about our relationship, Bram."

"Good." His smile returned, brimming with self-satisfaction. His seductive touch, as he ran a palm down her hair, was smooth and practiced.

She'd never thought it was going to be easy, Dani reminded herself. She stepped out from beneath his hand. "I don't think you understand."

He watched the walls going up around her, debated knocking them down, then decided to allow her to do this her way. For now. "Why don't you try me?" he suggested.

His tone was unthreatening, almost amiable. Perhaps, Dani considered, she'd misjudged Bram. Perhaps, despite what he'd said about wanting to sleep together, he'd spent the past three weeks—when he wasn't in Eden's bed, that is, she tacked on evilly—trying to figure a way out of this marriage without making it appear he was abandoning his dead brother's pregnant fiancée.

"I appreciate your motives in marrying me," she began slowly, carefully. "And I'm not going to lie and say that I'm not attracted to you, because I am.

"But," she said quickly when she saw triumph flash in his eyes, "I think entering into a physical relationship would only make things more difficult when we separate."

"Separate?" Her soft protest did not come as a surprise. He'd been expecting it since noticing the absence of her wedding band. But he hadn't expected it to cause such anger. Or such panic—a cold, metallic panic he could actually taste.

"I seem to recall, when we were standing in front of that judge in Las Vegas, saying something about 'until death do us part.'" He had no way of knowing that his words were the same ones that Peter had thrown at her as a threat.

She paled. "And I seem to recall you promising we'd get a divorce."

"After our baby's born," he reminded her. Although impatience continued to simmer through him, Bram surprised them both by smiling. "Until then, I'm afraid we're stuck with each other, sweetheart. For better or worse."

Dear Lord, he meant it, Dani realized. She'd definitely misjudged him, which proved yet again the mistake she'd made marrying a man she didn't know. A man she couldn't begin to understand.

Only a few weeks ago, Bram Fortune had been the quintessential bachelor. And now, was she supposed to suddenly believe that he was actually eager to play a starring role in a remake of "Father Knows Best"?

All her carefully rehearsed words, all her prepared arguments, flew out the window. She lifted her trembling hands to drag them through her hair, then let them fall.

"You have to understand."

"I'm trying." Although the uncharacteristic panic had abated, Bram wasn't at all certain what he was feeling. He was sure, however, that he'd never felt anything like it before.

Dani could hear the banked frustration in his voice. "This isn't easy for me," she said.

"I'm not sure it should be." Sighing, he slid his hand beneath her hair and began stroking the nape of her neck. "For either of us."

His kneading fingers created a soft mist that clouded her mind. How could she possibly explain to him what she was feeling? Dani wondered. When she didn't understand it herself?

Ancient fears, old resolutions, new desires, foolish wishes—they were all crowding in at her, so close Dani felt as if she'd surely suffocate.

It was only raging hormones that had her feeling so horrendously out of control, she assured herself.

When she slid away from his touch yet again, Bram let her go. She was, he reminded himself, more fragile than she looked. More fragile than she wanted to be.

Hoping to reassure her by putting a bit of distance between them, he walked the few feet to his desk and leaned against it.

"I'm not going to rush you into making love with me, Dani."

His hands were practically itching with the need to touch her. Bram reached into his shirt pocket for a much-needed cigarette, then remembered her morning sickness and the surgeon general's report on secondhand smoke.

Seeking something, anything for his hands to do, he picked up a hand-cut crystal paperweight. The Waterford crystal, in the shape of a baseball, had been a Christmas gift from Eclipse Studios two years ago after his movie depicting the romantic and professional trials of a washed-up pitcher had defied pessimistic studio bean counters with a blockbuster opening weekend. As he began idly stroking its flawlessly cut diamond facets with a fingertip, Bram reminded himself that when something fragile was handled clumsily, it could easily shatter.

Although he'd never considered patience his long suit, Bram was willing to try to rein in his own feelings. His own needs.

For Dani. For now.

"I'd just like you to start thinking about it."

His intelligent eyes saw too much. Too deep. Dani feared that the more Bram saw, the greater the chance was that he could gain an unwanted emotional hold on her.

"I don't think . . ." The confused emotions swelling up in her were so unbearably strong, all she could do was shake her head.

Feeling as if she was about to burst into tears, Dani closed her eyes. Her mind was clouded with thoughts too tangled to comprehend. Her heart was overwhelmed with emotions too complex to catalog. *Hormones*, she told herself. *Oh, God. Please let that be all it is.*

Her skin looked like parchment. Her eyes, when she opened them again, glistened. Bram wanted to kiss away the tears pooling at the corners of those stricken eyes, but pride and a lingering annoyance that the long-awaited evening should end in such a shambles kept him where he was.

"You've had a long day," he said, congratulating himself on his steady, rational voice when what he wanted to do was to yell at her, to curse her, to demand that she trust him not to hurt her as her son-of-a-bitch husband had done. "You should probably go upstairs and get some rest. You look tired."

Actually, she looked a hell of a lot more than tired. She was too pale, the smooth flesh beneath her eyes was smudged with purple shadows, she'd chewed off her bright lipstick and her hair was in an unruly mass of tangles from her having dragged her nervous hands through it.

Bram knew he was in deep, deep trouble because she still looked absolutely beautiful to him.

"What about you?"

Bram hated the way she was looking at him as if she was afraid he was going to drag her upstairs to his bed and rape her.

He shrugged. "I'm still wired from the flight. I think I'll go to the studio and see about getting some work done."

"Oh. Well." She was fingering the chain around her neck again. "I guess I'll see you in the morning?" Her voice went up a little, turning it into a question.

The lambent fear had faded from her eyes. In its place was the reluctant desire that caused a damnably familiar throbbing ache inside him. "You can count on it."

Damn her! She was looking at him with something that could only be disappointment. Didn't she realize that she was driving him crazy with these mixed messages?

The only thing to do was to leave her to herself, Bram realized. The way she kept insisting she wanted to be. He had to get out of here. Now. Before he forgot he was supposed to be a gentleman. Before he took her up on that reluctant feminine invitation that had begun to glow in her dark eyes.

He grabbed his jacket from the chair where he'd tossed it when he first came home. Then he walked away. Although it took a herculean effort, Bram resisted the urge to slam the door behind him.

Alone, as she'd insisted she wanted to be, Dani sank onto the couch. Her knees were trembling. Her entire body was trembling.

She sat there, her arms wrapped around herself, listening to the throaty purr of the Jaguar as the engine came to life. She stayed there, long after the sound of the car driving away had faded beneath the steady roar of the surf's constant ebb and flow.

Then, finally, much, much later, when she thought she could manage it, Dani climbed the stairs to the guest bedroom, where, after undressing, she curled up in a ball atop the mattress and wept for all of them.

For Ryan, for Bram, for herself, and, last but certainly not least, Dani wept for their innocent unborn child.

IT WAS NEARLY DAWN when Bram returned home, exhausted and even more frustrated than when he'd left.

He tried to remember the last time he hadn't been able to lose himself in his work, and came up blank. Even during those oppressive, dark days immediately following Ryan's accident, Bram had gone to the studio, operating as if on autopilot.

He'd worked nearly around the clock—eighteen, nineteen, sometimes twenty hours a day. In an effort to rid his heart and mind of the pain of his brother's death, he'd driven himself mercilessly, forcing himself to focus like a laser on *Scandals*, burying himself in the script and planning the trip to Thailand.

Work had been his respite. His salvation. His obsession. And now, having admitted to one obsession, Bram could recognize another.

It was, he admitted with a burst of frustrated anger, obsession that made him unable to concentrate. It was obsession that had him staring off into space, remembering all the things he'd done to Dani—with her—at the cabin, and fantasizing about all the things he had yet to do. Hot, erotic, scandalous things he was aching to do.

It wasn't going to work.

He knew he'd promised to give her time, but that was before he realized that the woman he'd married on a whim possessed the power to control his mind. And, more painfully, his body.

He wanted her, dammit. And she wanted him. So, as he entered the house, Bram decided that he was going to go upstairs, take a long hot shower to get rid of the frustration, sweat and cigarette smoke clinging to his skin and then, he was going to do his damnedest to seduce his wife.

And if he couldn't pull that off, he considered as he climbed the stairs, yanking the sweater over his head as he went, then he wasn't the man he'd always known himself to be.

He was headed toward the bathroom, when some deep-seated instinct drew him into the room Dani had commandeered as a studio. It smelled of turpentine and paint. Along with that aroma of her work, her floral scent lingered, teasing the senses.

Moonlight and star shine streamed in through the skylights, making the room almost as bright as day. A few canvases—ones that apparently hadn't made the cut for the showing—were leaning against a wall. On an easel, a newly stretched canvas waited for Dani's inspiration to fill it with life and color.

This was the one place where she'd allowed her emotions free rein, and although he suspected it was merely his writer's admittedly vivid imagination working overtime, Bram could almost feel a bit of her creative energy, a living, crackling force.

She'd left a sketch pad on a nearby table. The price sticker on the cover bore the name of a Malibu art-supply store, suggesting that she'd purchased the pad recently.

With no ulterior motive in mind, Bram began idly flipping the pages. What he found hit him like a punch to the gut.

Ryan's face smiled back at Bram on page after page. Ryan of the serious, warm eyes. Ryan of the shy, boyish smile. Ryan the Boy Scout. Ryan the Benevolent. Sir Ryan the Good; Bram had teased him unmercifully during their adolescent years.

The charcoal sketches revealed a depth of emotion so strong that Bram found himself torn between misery and jealousy. He had never doubted Dani's love for his younger brother. But never had he realized it burned quite so intensely. Ryan Fortune had been the brilliant sun around which Dani's entire life had revolved.

Bram closed the pad. And his eyes. He took a deep breath, only to experience a sharp, stabbing pain that reminded him all too vividly of a time when he was fourteen and had fallen off his motorbike, knocking the wind out of his lungs.

He couldn't breathe then. And he couldn't breathe now.

He couldn't think. Or move. He felt as if he was locked in a freeze-frame.

His hands ached. Glancing down, Bram realized that his fingers had curled into tight, painful fists, as if needing to strike out at someone.

But at whom? Not Ryan, certainly. What kind of selfish bastard could be jealous of a dead man? Especially when that man was his own brother?

Neither could Bram blame Dani for this cold black hole he felt himself being sucked into. How could he condemn her for remaining loyal to the man she loved? Even after death?

It was at that moment that all the unsettling feelings Bram had been experiencing since making illicit love to his brother's fiancée came crashing into place.

He'd been wrong last night. He was not in danger of falling in love with Dani. He'd already fallen and had landed flat on the ground. Hard.

Cursing, Bram dragged his hand down his face, trying to sort out emotions that were both painful and unfamiliar. Returning the sketch pad to the table, he left the room and crossed the hallway to the guest room. The door squeaked slightly when he opened it, but Dani, exhausted by her long and emotional day, remained dead to the world.

From the way she'd kicked off the sheets, Bram suspected that Dani's mind was as restless as his. She was lying on her side, curled up into a tight ball, as if she'd cried herself to sleep. Both slender hands were beneath her cheek; her hair was loose, spilling over her pillow like an ebony waterfall.

The slender gold chain was still around her neck. Knowing—dreading—what he'd find, Bram couldn't stop himself from bending down and lightly pulling it from beneath the neckline of the nightshirt.

The familiar diamond solitaire caught the streaming moonlight, trapping it in its perfect facets, turning it to brilliant ice.

As he held his brother's ring in his hand, Bram felt himself drowning in a deep, dark pool of desolation.

Bram Fortune had garnered both fame and fortune by chronicling all the moods of love. He'd carved out a very successful niche for himself by writing screenplays exploring the dark side of that illusive, powerful emotion.

In a Fortune film, couples in love were known to lie, cheat, betray one another, and sometimes, as in his current project, were even driven to kill. A Fortune film was not, as critic Roger Ebert had once pointed out, even while giving Bram an enthusiastic thumbs-up, a very good "date" movie.

Nevertheless, moviegoers continually showed their approval of Bram's unique artistic vision by flocking to his films in droves. While critics inevitably praised his intricate layering of complex, often-dangerous emotions.

But for all his supposed insight on the subject, Bram had never suspected that love could hurt like this.

He'd never known that he could hurt like this.

11

THE NEXT MORNING, Dani made her wary way downstairs. But instead of the glowering husband she'd feared, she found a pot of freshly brewed coffee, a pitcher of orange juice and a note from Bram taped to the front of the microwave. He hoped she'd had a good sleep and, since *Scandals* was now in the editing process, he'd be working late at the studio.

Oh, a hastily scribbled postscript added, he hoped she had a nice day.

And that was it. Brief, formal and to the point. No veiled words of censure for having pricked his male ego, no warm words of affection to his bride. He'd even signed it simply, "Bram." She should be grateful, Dani told herself as she sipped the coffee and roamed the quiet and strangely lonely beach house. She hadn't been looking forward to another argument about their marital status. She should feel relieved that Bram appeared no more eager than she to dive into those turbulent conversational waters. She should, dammit. So why didn't she?

Unreasonably anxious and needing to work off some of her nervous energy, she spent the morning puttering around the house, changing the water in the tulips, adding scented oil to the potpourri, putting the ivy-sprigged shelf paper she'd purchased on a whim in all the kitchen cupboards. Dani did not question that such an action was impractical, considering she still had no intention of staying here for the duration of her pregnancy.

Indeed, she'd awakened this morning more determined than ever to make Bram see the light. To convince him that this farce of a marriage would never work. Now that her intended conversation had been forestalled, Dani assured herself that she was simply measuring and cutting shelf paper to keep busy. The mindless domestic chores kept her from having to think.

After a light lunch, she went out for a walk on the beach. The day had dawned as bright and sunny as a photograph on the cover of a Malibu tourist-bureau brochure. The vast waters of the Pacific Ocean glistened like liquid sapphire; overhead, sea gulls whirred and dived headlong into the waves, emerging seconds later with a splash of silver fish in their beaks.

A pair of mahogany-dark and stunningly fit young women in their early twenties lay stretched out on reed mats, oblivious to any reported dangers concerning lengthy sun exposure. A jogger ran along the water's edge, stopping every so often to check his time on his watch while a photographer took photos of a family of dolphins playing in the sunlit sea.

An old man in faded denim shorts, and a Save The Whales T-shirt walked along the sand, picking up seashells, while a young boy's crimson dragon kite rose higher and higher into the cloudless blue sky.

Normally, such an idyllic, convivial scene would have lifted Dani's spirits. But today, as she trudged along the water-hardened sand at the edge of the surf, trying to convince herself that she was glad Bram had left early for the studio, she couldn't help wondering if he was using his work as an excuse to avoid her.

Perhaps, she mused unhappily, Bram had decided to take advantage of her willingness to end their marriage. Perhaps he was even relieved to have an excuse to wash his hands of her.

But if an annulment was truly what she wanted, why did that idea make her feel so bad?

"Lord," she muttered, "why don't you make up your mind? No wonder men claim they can't understand women."

Dani wanted Bram. And she didn't want him. Then she did. But even when she did, she didn't want to want him. Her mind and her emotions kept bouncing back and forth, like a tennis ball caught in an endless volley.

Hormones, she hoped yet again.

Immersed in her tumultuous thoughts as she returned to the house after her brisk walk, Dani failed to notice that the photographer's high-powered telescopic lens was now trained on her.

By the time the sun had set into the bright waters outside the windows, her vague depression had changed to irritation. If Bram Fortune believed she was going to spend these next months sitting idly around his house, hoping for him to deign to spend time with his wife, he had another think coming!

She'd had a full and busy life before Bram Fortune. And she'd have one after him. Her life, she assured herself, did not revolve around some egotistical workaholic. Even if he was a world-class kisser.

She worked herself up into a temper, marching into her studio, where she spent the next hour throwing paint onto her new canvas, and rehearsing all the mean, hateful, hurtful things she was going to say to Bram when he did finally show up, when an unexpected delivery arrived at the door.

"I didn't order any dinner," she insisted after the soap-opera-gorgeous young man had explained what he was carrying in the insulated bags.

"Your husband ordered this, Mrs. Fortune." A brilliant smile revealed a row of teeth so straight and gleaming white they could only be caps. During her short time in southern California, Dani had come to the conclusion that nearly every waiter, salesclerk, bus driver and gas-station attendant was an out-of-work actor.

Still in a snit, and irritated that Bram would think she wasn't capable of feeding herself, Dani was tempted to refuse the delivery. But the aromas wafting from the package tempted.

"What is it?" she asked reluctantly, horribly afraid she was perched on the slippery precipice of surrender.

"Crawfish *étouffée*, jambalaya, shrimp gumbo and tequila Key-lime pie. Oh, and pralines, of course."

"Of course," Dani murmured, even as her mouth watered.

The toothpaste-commercial smile flashed again. "From Papa Joe's Ragin' Cajun Café on Melrose. Home of the best Cajun food west of Nwahluns."

Dani caved, as she—and Bram, dammit—had known she would. "Come on in."

After overtipping the deliveryman, she began opening the bags. In the first one she found a short note, written in Bram's bold strong script.

"*Bon appétit*," she read. "Hope this is spicy enough to satisfy any pregnancy cravings." Along with the note was an audiocassette of Cajun music. For atmosphere, the accompanying note suggested.

The zydeco music, which reminded Dani of juiced-up country, did indeed prove to be a perfect accompaniment for the savory meal, which only served to irritate her further. If he was going to ignore her, the least Bram could do was not confuse her by being so damn thoughtful!

And Papa Joe's cuisine did satisfy her seemingly constant yearning for spicy food. But, unfortunately, as she climbed the stairs hours later, Dani had to admit that Bram's meal did nothing for that other, more elemental craving.

Much later, unable to fall asleep, she went back into the studio, picked up her sketch pad and began to draw. But she couldn't keep her mind on her work. Not when, as impossible as she knew it to be, Dani could sense Bram's presence in the moonlit room.

Tired and keyed up all at the same time, she dragged herself to bed, where she lay staring up at the ceiling, waiting for the sound of Bram's Jaguar to pull into the drive.

She was to have a very long wait.

For five long and frustratingly lonely days, Dani's only contact with Bram was through the notes he left her on the microwave, the refrigerator, the bathroom mirror. Or the brief messages on the telephone recorder. And the dinner he arranged to have delivered each night. Although she'd left her own note telling him that she was perfectly capable of feeding herself, he wrote back that he didn't want her to wear herself out cooking. That settled to his satisfaction, the meals continued to arrive every night at six-thirty like clockwork.

Frustrated and still too creatively drained from her rush to get the paintings finished in time for her show to return to work full time, Dani decided that if she didn't find something to do, she'd go stark raving mad.

Desperate for human company, she was more than a little grateful when Arturo dropped by to invite her to a late lunch.

"I'm so restless," she complained over a delicious crab-and-pasta salad at the Bistro Garden. "I'm not really ready to start a new series of paintings, but if I don't find something to do . . ." Her voice drifted off in frustration.

"I've just the thing for you," Arturo assured her. "Do you remember meeting Madeline Hartlove at your show?"

"Madeline Hartlove," Dani repeated, her mind running through the sea of faces Arturo and Dennis had introduced her to that night. "Late forties, society-girl ash blond hair, blue eyes, Scaasi cocktail dress with very good diamonds?"

"That's her," Arturo confirmed. "She runs a shelter," he revealed. "The Anchorage. It's a halfway house for battered women."

Dani's blood chilled. Her fingers tightened on her salad fork. "I don't think—"

The gallery owner deftly ignored her faint, planned protest. "Madeline was telling me just this morning that she was looking for some project for the residents to do. Something that would boost their self-esteem."

"Well, I wish her luck." Dani took a long drink of ice water in an attempt to soothe her nerves.

"Luck always helps," he agreed easily as he buttered a poppyseed roll. "But you and I both know that sometimes it's not enough." He looked at her expectantly.

Dani shook her head. "It was hard enough to save my own life, Arturo," she reminded him. Besides her therapist and the team of San Francisco doctors that healed her wounds and put her face back together, Arturo and Dennis were the only two people—with the exception of Ryan, of course—who knew what she'd suffered. "I don't have the strength to save the world."

"Madeline isn't asking for the world, Dani." He put the roll down on the flowered plate and reached across the table and covered her hand with his. "All she's asking, dear heart, is for a little help in her quest to help others."

"Are you suggesting I give art lessons?"

"Art therapy has proved very helpful in a lot of cases," he said, telling her what she already knew. "And who knows, maybe you'll have the pleasure of discovering a true talent. But even those who'll never be Picasso or Jackson Pollock or even Grandma Moses will have gotten some measure of relief from putting their horrors—and their hopes—on canvas."

Having had enough horrors of her own to last a lifetime, Dani was not at all eager to relive any of them. Or to share in anyone else's. But it was Arturo's comment about hope that garnered her reluctant attention.

She'd been lucky enough to have Ryan. How could she deny other women—women who were in that unholy place where she'd once been—a similar chance to rejoin the human race?

"Madeline Hartlove," she murmured. "I suppose the number for the shelter is in the phone book?"

"You're in luck," Arturo said with an unrepentant, knowing grin. "I just happen to have her card with me."

As she took the white card from his outstretched hand, Dani felt a lot like Eve, accepting that shiny red apple from the serpent in the garden.

She'd no sooner slipped the business card into her purse when she glanced up and saw Bram approaching. Heads swiveled as he passed each table. A buzz of excited conversation followed him.

"Hello, sweetheart." Appearing unaware of the attention he'd drawn, Bram bent down and gave her a husbandly peck on the cheek.

Irked by his recent disappearing act, Dani didn't respond. If Bram was annoyed by her refusal to return his greeting, he didn't show it.

"Arturo." He smiled at the gallery owner. "It's good to see you again."

"I'm delighted to see you. I do hope you're enjoying our Dani's painting."

"Almost as much as I enjoy Dani." He ran his palm over her shoulder in a light, possessive gesture.

Dani shrugged off his touch. "What are you doing here, Bram?" she asked, almost choking on the bitterness in her throat.

She'd known going in that they were only marrying for appearance' sake, but how could he stand there and behave as if they were normal newlyweds? As if he was glad to see her?

"Looking for you, of course."

Chilling memories of Peter stalking her all over San Francisco, watching her every move, caused a flare of hot anger mixed with ice to surge through her veins. "How did you find me?"

Bram watched her spine stiffen. *Ghosts*, he thought. The lady had more than her share. "I figured, when you weren't at home, that you might have gone to the gallery." Bram kept his voice purposefully casual. "Dennis told me that you and Arturo were having lunch." He treated them both to his friendliest smile, pulled up a chair and sat down beside her.

Dani believed him. Her heart, which had sunk to her stomach like a stone, began to beat again. "Why don't you join us?" No longer frightened, she was still piqued by his recent absence.

"Thanks." Her sarcasm rolled off his back like rain off the sleekly waxed finish of his Jaguar. "But I don't really have time for lunch." He glanced down at his watch. "Since your monthly doctor's appointment is in twenty minutes."

Once again, paranoia lifted its ugly head. "How did you know about that?"

Lord, she was suspicious, Bram considered, tamping down his own irritation. The one thing he didn't want to do was cause another scene. Not when his brawl with Bannister had already made the cover of this week's *Inquisitor.*

From Dani's chilly reception, Bram decided she'd yet to see the supermarket tabloid. If she had, given her flash-fire temper, she probably would have started throwing china the minute she'd seen the whites of his eyes.

"You wrote it on the kitchen calendar," he reminded her.

"Oh." He had her there. "Well, what does that have to do with you?"

"I intend to take you, of course."

"That isn't necessary."

"Of course, it is." He picked up her water glass and turned it to where the edge of the crystal was stained with a smudge of vermilion lipstick. With his eyes still on hers, he drank from that same spot, the gesture both proprietary and unbelievably sensual.

"I'm your husband," he said. "It's my child you're carrying."

"Child?" Arturo piped up, his voice trilling with interest. "Dani? More secrets?"

He could have been invisible, the way both Dani and Bram were ignoring him.

"*Our* child." Dani scowled as she threw Bram's initial correction back in his face.

"Exactly." He returned the glass to the table, leaned back in the chair and crossed his arms. "Which is why I have every intention of discussing your condition with your doctor." His tone suggested that he considered the argument closed.

"Oh, really?" She leaned forward, braced her elbows on the linen tablecloth, linked her fingers together and rested her chin on them. "And what, may I ask, brought about this sudden concern for my well-being?"

"It's not sudden at all. Actually, I've had several long and enlightening conversations with Dr. Marshall. I just felt, now that I'm back home, it was time we met in person."

"You've talked with my doctor?" Dani sputtered. "While you were in Thailand? About me?"

"Of course. Did you actually believe I'd go running off to the jungle without ensuring that you were being well cared for?"

At this point, Dani didn't know what to believe about Bram Fortune. Every time she thought she had him figured out, he threw her another curve.

When she didn't answer, he cast another significant glance at his watch. "We'd better get going. Wouldn't want to keep the good doctor waiting." He stood. "You will excuse us, won't you, Arturo?"

"Of course." The gallery owner had been avidly observing the subdued argument, his head turning back and forth between Dani and Bram as if he were a spectator at a heated match on Wimbledon's Centre Court. "It was grand seeing you again, Bram. I can tell Dani's in excellent hands."

Ignoring Dani's muffled curse, Arturo scribbled his name on the American Express charge slip, then rose, as well. He kissed her on the cheek. "I'll tell Madeline you'll be calling."

"You do that," she muttered through set teeth, furious at the way both men had managed to manipulate her yet again.

As they drove the few blocks to the Sunset Boulevard office in silence, Dani was fuming. Bram could practically see the puffs of smoke coming out of the top of her head.

"I hope you're not going to sulk all evening," he said into the thick silence surrounding them.

"I'm not sulking."

But she was. And they both knew it. Unfazed, Bram was whistling as he pulled into the parking garage. "Who's Madeline?" he asked as they entered the white-stucco medical building.

"A friend of Arturo's. I may do some volunteer work with her." Dani braced herself for Bram's autocratic disapproval.

"Sounds great. It'll do you good to get out of the house," Bram said as they entered the elevator. "You'll have to tell me all about it." He pushed the button for the sixth floor. The car began to rise. "Over dinner."

"Dinner?"

"Didn't I tell you? I thought I'd cook tonight."

"You're kidding."

"Actually, I'm a pretty fair chef. Admittedly I'm not as good as Papa Joe, but—"

"I was merely surprised that you were actually going to be home before midnight."

He arched a brow. "You sound as if you've missed me."

"Not at all," she lied. "What's the matter, Bram? Is Eden washing her hair tonight?"

"What does Eden have to do with you and I having dinner at home?"

She hadn't meant to even bring the subject up. But now that she had, she decided to get the matter of his mistress off her chest. "I can't help wondering if the reason you're never home is because you'd rather be with her."

"I told you the day we got married that my affair with Eden was over."

"That's what you told me. But the two of you certainly appeared close enough in Bangkok."

Damn. He'd worried about that blasted photographer at the time. Especially after Eden's PR flack called and told her the picture had aired on "ET." At the time Bram had opted not to mention it to Dani. After all, he'd told himself, foolishly it seemed, the chances of her actually seeing it were slim.

"Eden went out that night with some of the crew. Believe it or not, I was back at the hotel, trying to get through to you. Apparently things got pretty wild and they ended up getting separated. She called me from some strip joint, drunker than a skunk, begging me to come get her. What was I supposed to do? Leave her to get raped? Or worse?"

"Knowing your penchant for playing the white knight, I almost believe you," Dani allowed.

"You should. Because all that happened was that I dragged her to her suite, poured her into bed, then went back to trying to call my wife. Who I missed very much.

"And for the record," he added, "as to my staying away these past days, I received the impression, the first night I returned home from Thailand, that you'd just as soon I leave you alone."

"You're the one who insisted we stay married," Dani reminded grumpily.

"Until after the baby's born," he said.

"Well, it would have been nice if you'd told me going into this arrangement that I was marrying Houdini."

Bram felt a burst of masculine satisfaction. She was angry. With him. Reminding himself that an angry woman was not an indifferent one, he put his arm around her waist as they walked together down the hallway.

"I really have been swamped with work," he told her. It was the truth. Just not the entire truth. "But I promise, from now on, things are going to change."

"What does that mean?" She didn't know whether to take his words as a promise or a threat.

"It means that I intend to rectify the situation. Beginning tonight."

"By cooking dinner?"

"I figure that's a start," Bram said as he ushered her into the office filled with women. "After that, we'll just have to play it by ear."

As they waited to see the doctor, Bram idly leafed through a magazine, steadfastly ignoring, Dani noticed, the openly speculative glances of more than one visibly pregnant woman.

She'd thought the looks were born of feminine interest. But a tabloid newspaper, left behind by a former patient in the examining room, suggested that there was another reason she and Bram had been the center of attention.

Her temper predictably flared. She tore the cover page off the paper and stuffed it into her purse. With effort, Dani held her ire in check during the examination. Since Bram insisted on meeting with the doctor afterward, Dani had to wait to wave the unattractive headline in his face. Such uncharacteristic patience served its purpose. By the time they exited the medical building, she was no longer mad enough to chew nails.

"I thought it went quite well," Bram said, as he drove to Malibu.

"If you can call being lectured about weight gain going well," she replied, scowling about the suggestion to cut down on the ice cream.

"Don't worry about it." Bram shrugged. "The doctor said you were still well within the accepted range."

"For a water buffalo," she muttered. The unhappy truth was, she'd been appalled as she'd watched the weight moving farther and farther up the scale.

"For a pregnant woman," he corrected easily. "And for the record, I think you look terrific. Besides, Ryan and I were both big babies. Most of whatever weight you've gained is probably just Junior."

Dani appreciated his efforts to lift her mood. She'd accepted the idea of an expanding waistline; indeed, she was actually secretly thrilled about the changes in her body, knowing that they were the result of a new life growing inside her.

She still didn't exactly look pregnant, she'd thought that morning, studying herself critically in the bathroom mirror. Not yet. But she was beginning to look fat. As she'd pulled her knit top tight against her stomach, Dani couldn't help wondering if Bram found her recent weight gain a turnoff.

After all, what red-blooded American male, when given a choice between going to bed with Eden Vail or a fat, hormonally crazy wife, wouldn't pick the actress? The difference between Bram and all the other men in the world was that he actually had the opportunity.

The problem was, Dani was forced to consider, if she really didn't want Bram to want her, then why did she care whether or not he still found her attractive? Why did she feel such a flash of primal female jealousy whenever she thought of Eden Vail?

"Thank you," she murmured. "For the words of encouragement," she explained at his sideways, questioning glance.

"Any time," Bram offered amiably. "I figure it's the least I can do, since I'm half responsible and you're the one who suffered through morning sickness and is still facing all the hard work down the line."

He frowned as he asked the question that had been nagging at him too much lately. "Are you sorry you're pregnant?"

"It'd be a little late to be sorry," she told him. Realizing it wasn't the answer Bram wanted, and deciding that there was no point in holding back such an important truth, she said, "When I first found out, I was stunned. And a little angry."

"That's probably a normal enough reaction," Bram agreed. He wanted to ask if she was still angry with him, but since they were actually managing to have a civil conversation, decided not to.

"I suppose so." She pressed her hands against her stomach. Some days it still floored her that a baby—her and Bram's baby—was growing inside her. She mentally shook off the unexpected prick of guilt that it wasn't Ryan's child she was carrying. "Then I was scared."

"Of the pain?"

"No. Well, naturally, I'm not looking forward to that, but mostly I was afraid that I wouldn't be a good mother. That I wouldn't know what to do."

"Every parent makes mistakes." Bram shrugged. "Yours did. Mine did. And look how well we managed to turn out," he said with a dashing grin that earned a smile in return.

A comfortable silence settled over them as they passed the UCLA campus. Dani thought about showing him the tabloid page she'd taken from the examining room and decided that they were getting along too well to bring up such an unpleasant subject. They'd have to discuss it, she knew. But later. After dinner, perhaps.

"I appreciated you coming with me today," she said.

The truth was, she'd felt proud to have Bram sitting beside her. Not many women in the waiting room had been accompanied by their husbands. And the husbands that were there were obviously uncomfortable to be surrounded by so many visibly pregnant women, while Bram appeared to take it in stride.

There was another reason she'd felt a burst of purely wifely pride, Dani admitted. And that was because her husband was so distractingly good-looking. There hadn't been a man in the room who'd even come close.

"Next time we'll have to remember to take a *Newsweek* along." Dani smiled, thinking how odd it had seemed watching Bram reading that outdated issue of *Parents* magazine. Odd, but rather sweet. "Or *Variety*."

"Actually, some of the articles were kind of interesting." They'd reached the beach. Beyond the golden sand, the long shallow crescent of Santa Monica Bay swept north toward Malibu. "In fact, while you were being examined, I read one comparing breast-feeding with bottle-feeding."

He slanted her a sideways glance as he stopped at the intersection before turning onto the traffic-jammed Pacific Coast Highway. "Have you decided which you're going to do?"

Although they'd already been intimate enough to make a child together, for some reason Dani found the topic embarrassing. "I want to try to breast-feed."

Bram watched the color rise in her cheeks. His gaze moved to her breasts and lingered there for a long, suspended moment.

"I'm glad." His husky voice vibrated up her nerve endings. "The article said breast milk is best."

Although she knew it was impossible, Dani imagined that she actually could feel Bram's firmly shaped lips scorching her unusually sensitive flesh. "That's what the doctor said, too," she agreed softly.

Their eyes met. And held. Exchanging intimate messages.
"Dani—"

"Yes?"

"We need to talk."

"Yes." Her voice was throaty with pent-up emotion. As she leaned toward him, Dani's lips parted in feminine invitation.

His mouth was a whisper away and Dani was holding an expectant breath when the sudden impatient blare of a car horn behind them shattered the moment.

Bram cursed and shot a murderous glance in the rearview mirror as he pulled out into the intersection. Unable to help herself, Dani began to laugh. And laugh.

"I don't really think it was all that funny," Bram muttered as they continued up the winding coast road.

"It wasn't," Dani admitted, wiping at the tears streaming down her face with the back of her hand. "Not really." She bit her lip and took a deep breath, struggling for calm. "It's only hormones," she explained. "They swing all over the place these days."

"I read an article about that, too," Bram said obligingly. It had, he considered, explained a great deal about Dani's recent ambivalent behavior.

"But—" she choked, then recovered "—if you could have only seen your face..." At the memory of Bram's hot frustration, she burst into another gale of giggles.

It was the first time he'd heard her laugh since they were kids. Listening to the bright, musical sound that pulled at a thousand hidden chords inside him, Bram understood all too well why Ryan had fallen in love with Dani Cantrell.

What was more difficult to figure out, Bram considered as he pulled into the driveway of the beach house, was why, when she'd been under his nose for most of his life, it had taken him so long.

12

AFTER CHANGING INTO a pair of jeans, which, if she lay on her back on the bed to zip them and didn't fasten the top snap, still fit, and a scarlet tunic sweater, Dani went back downstairs. There, perched on a bar stool in the kitchen, she sipped a cup of orange spiced tea and watched Bram prepare scampi and angel-hair pasta with a deft economy of motion she couldn't help but admire. Outside the windows, a crimson sun was sinking into the sapphire blue sea, turning the water to gleaming gold.

To Dani's vast relief the dinner went amazingly smoothly. Once again she debated showing Bram the tabloid. Once again, she put it off. It would undoubtedly make him furious and she hated the idea of spoiling such a rare, uncomplicated evening.

He told her about the editing process, and how it looked as if they were going to have to loop some of the dialogue from the jungle scenes in the studio. He did not mention that today, as he'd driven through the studio gates, one of the picketers had thrown a rock at his car. Although the stone hadn't done any damage—it merely glanced off his windshield—it had made him angry as hell. An anger that had abated when he'd walked into the restaurant and seen his gorgeous wife.

When she told him about Arturo's suggestion that she volunteer at the shelter, Bram proved supportive.

"So long as you don't wear yourself out," he added, which she chose to take as normal husbandly concern, rather than any ulterior motivation to control her life. As Peter had done.

"Don't worry." She stood, prepared to clear the table. "I won't do anything that might endanger the baby."

"I didn't think you would," Bram said easily. "What do you think you're doing?"

"You did the cooking. I'm going to do the dishes."

"It'll take me ten minutes to finish things up in here." Bram rose as well, and took the plate from her hand.

"I'm not an invalid," she reminded him.

"Of course you're not." Indeed, he'd felt a vast sense of relief when the doctor had assured them that Dani was in excellent health.

"So, why won't you let me help?"

"Because I know how hard you worked getting ready for your show, and because I think you've earned a rest. Besides, a pregnant woman deserves pampering."

She lifted an ebony brow. "In case you've been too busy working in the world of make-believe to have noticed, Bram, society has progressed beyond the Victorian age."

"So sue me," Bram said with an unapologetic shrug. "It's the way I feel. Oh," he said as a thought occurred to him, "I almost forgot." He stopped gathering up the dishes long enough to go over to the desk and open his alligator briefcase.

"You bought me a present?" Dani asked as he handed her the package wrapped in white paper and tied with a gilt ribbon. "Why?"

"Can't a man buy his wife a present just because he feels like it?"

"What is it?" An unwelcome memory of her honeymoon slipped into her mind, when Peter had returned to the suite with those emeralds. And there had been other gifts, other apologies from her husband for having struck her.

"Why don't you open it and see?"

She was turning the small box around and around in her hands. "You didn't have to do this."

"Hey, it's not that big a deal." His smile and his eyes revealed patient amusement. "I was just thinking of you today, Dani, so I stopped by Macy's on the way to the restaurant and picked this up."

And waited in line to have it gift wrapped, Dani considered as she slipped the gold ribbon off. As she saw the familiar floral packaging, she smiled. "Bubble bath."

"In your scent. I thought after dinner, while I cleaned up the kitchen, you might like to take a nice long bath."

She wanted to complain that he was trying to manipulate her again. But an annoying ache had been nagging at her back all day. A long soak in a warm bath sounded like nirvana.

She folded, as she suspected he'd known all along she would. "All right, Bram. You win. I'll go soak in the tub while you do the damn dishes." She tossed her head with a final, mostly feigned flare of rebellion. "Satisfied?"

"I've been a helluva long way from satisfied since I put you on that plane on our wedding night, sweetheart." His smile faded, his voice turned gruff with unsatiated desire.

Dani didn't answer; Bram hadn't expected her to.

However, after she'd gone upstairs, he muttered a vicious curse, took several deep breaths that did nothing to ease the near-constant ache in his groin, and reminded himself that some things—some people—were worth waiting for.

Nearly forty-five minutes later, the last of Dani's annoyance had been soothed away by the whirlpool jets of Bram's enormous tub. Feeling as loose as wet spaghetti, she wrapped herself in an oversize towel and returned to the guest room.

She wasn't particularly surprised to find Bram waiting for her. But when she saw he was holding the tabloid page, her sense of well-being fled.

"Where did you get that?"

She looked warm and flushed and delicious. Bram indulged himself with a fleeting fantasy of slowly unwrapping her from those voluminous folds of navy terry cloth.

"I wasn't searching through your purse," he assured her.

"I didn't think you were." It was the truth. That was something Peter would have done. But not Bram.

"It was on the counter and I accidentally knocked it over. This piece of garbage fell out." His jaw was tight. His eyes more wary than angry. "How long have you known?"

"Since this afternoon. Someone left it in the examining room."

"I'm surprised you didn't hit the roof."

She surprised him by smiling. A soft little smile that seemed to be directed inward. "It's a little difficult to work up a decent fury when you're dressed in a horrid paper gown that doesn't begin to cover the essentials."

"Why didn't you mention it later? In the car? Or during dinner?"

"I intended to. But we were getting along so well, I hated spoiling the mood."

"Don't feel like the Lone Ranger."

Her eyes widened. "Are you saying—?"

"I kept putting it off, too."

And here she'd worried that she was going to have to break the news to him! "When did *you* find out?"

"The minute the damn thing came out this morning my phone started ringing. By the time I walked in that restaurant this afternoon, I half expected you to throw something at me."

"Why would I be angry at you?"

"If I hadn't punched the bastard, we probably wouldn't have made the front page."

She glanced down at the photo of Bram standing over her former husband. The photographer had managed to catch her in the shot as well, her hand over her mouth, her eyes as huge as saucers.

Dani shrugged her bare shoulders. "It's all blood under the bridge. Besides," she admitted, "you only did what I've wanted to do for years. In fact, when I first saw the picture, I was furious. Then I realized that every grocery shopper in America is going to see Peter bleeding all over his shirt-front."

"The guy's an instant celebrity," Bram agreed. "Hollywood-style."

"The shock waves reverberating through the Bannister-family mansion are probably going off the Richter scale."

Peter's haughty society parents had always treated her like an interloper, a commoner who wasn't good enough to marry their illustrious only son. Thinking about how they must be reacting to this unflattering fame made Dani grin.

"I just have one question."

"What's that?" Bram asked absently, staring at the way her dazzling smile lit up her entire face. Lord, she was lovely!

"If an ex-husband falls in the forest and a tabloid reporter isn't there to hear him, does he make a sound?"

Bram chuckled, relieved that the altercation he'd been expecting over the story wasn't going to happen. "Beats me." He wadded the page into a tight ball and tossed it into the wicker wastebasket across the room. "Are you upset about the news of our marriage getting out?"

"It was bound to, eventually." A thought occurred to her. "I wonder why the phone's been quiet all night."

"My service is picking up the calls. I didn't want us to be interrupted."

"Oh." Dani knew Bram was referring more to their overdue discussion than their surprisingly cordial dinner.

She looked and smelled like an angel. Knowing he couldn't stay in the same bedroom with Dani without needing to make love to her, Bram reluctantly stood.

"I'll wait downstairs on the deck. Then we can talk."

Dani nodded, not entirely trusting her voice.

She threw on a fleecy amethyst sweat suit, oversize orange-and-purple-striped socks and a pair of high-top sneakers and joined him out on the deck.

She was nervous. More than nervous. She looked, Bram considered, as if she were about to face a firing squad. He considered asking if she'd like a blindfold and a last cigarette, then decided she probably wouldn't appreciate the humor.

He stood and handed her a cup of tea in a thick earthenware mug. "Another cliché proven true," he murmured.

"What's that?" His slow appreciative smile had her toes curling.

"Not only were you a lovely bride, but you're living, breathing proof that pregnant women are gorgeous, too."

She ran a hand over her no-longer-flat stomach. "I should have known better than to marry a man with Irish blood flowing in his veins," she murmured. His gleaming gaze was making her feel unreasonably self-conscious. "Tell me, Bram, is it true that you have to bend over backward to kiss the Blarney stone?"

"Actually, it is. But anything I tell you isn't blarney, Dani." He sat back down on the deck swing and patted the seat, inviting her to join him. "It's the truth." His face was cast in shadow, but she could hear the sincerity in his voice. "I'd never lie to you."

"I know." With a soft, rippling sigh, she sat down beside him. The moon came out from behind a dark cloud. Bram and Dani sat there, swinging lightly, looking out at the shimmering silver path on the ebony water.

When Bram reached out to take her hand, Dani didn't pull away. "You're wearing your wedding ring." His finger brushed against the gold metal. "Since it's the first time I've seen you wear it since I returned home, I'd have to guess you wore it to prevent unwanted speculation at the doctor's."

Since he'd promised never to lie to her, Dani felt she owed Bram the same consideration. "I did."

"But you're still wearing it." His caressing touch was creating little sparks of heat. His gaze warmed her to the core.

"I know." When she'd gone to take it off before her bath, Dani had discovered that she really didn't want to. Wearing the simple gold band had, for the first time since her hastily arranged marriage, seemed incredibly right.

His hand moved across the back of her hand, and then up her arm, roving along her shoulder. His fingertips began stroking her neck. "You're not wearing Ryan's ring."

"You knew?"

After slipping Bram's ring onto her finger, Dani had felt strangely adulterous wearing his brother's ring on the gold chain around her neck. Putting her engagement ring away had proved horribly difficult and if Arturo hadn't arrived when he did, she undoubtedly would have spent the day in tears.

"I knew." Another black cloud drifted across the moon, once again throwing Bram's face into shadow, preventing Dani from reading his expression.

She swallowed. "I'm sorry. I didn't mean—"

"You don't have to explain." He picked up a glass from the wrought-iron table beside the swing and took a sip of brandy. "You told me from the start that you loved Ryan," he reminded her. For not the first time since marrying Dani, Bram experienced the dual pains of guilt and jealousy. "And that you probably always would."

Dani drew a careful breath and turned her head to stare out to sea. A very strong part of her longed to assure Bram that her feelings for his brother were in the past. But she couldn't. Because such a declaration would be a lie.

"The thing is," Bram said with studied casualness, "is that I've discovered I have this funny quirk."

She glanced warily at him over the rim of her mug. "What quirk is that?"

"When I love someone, I'd kind of like to have them love me back."

"*Love?*" The unexpected word came crashing down on her like a tidal wave. She shook her head, partly in denial, partly in an attempt to clear it. "But, you can't love me."

"Why not?" He took another sip of brandy. "You're not exactly unlovable, Dani."

Heaven help her, he appeared to be absolutely serious. Dani's mind spun, trying to sort out the thoughts that were tumbling through it.

"Any feelings you have for me are undoubtedly directed toward the mother of your child," she argued.

"That's what I tried telling myself. And for a time it was almost working. Until I realized that I began to feel something for you that night in the cabin. The first time we made love."

Even through her whirling senses, it did not escape Dani's attention that Bram had said "the first time" as if he were sure there would be others.

"But . . ." A woman was supposed to say something when a man professed his love. Dani knew that. But heaven help her, she literally couldn't think of any words, let alone the ones she suspected he was waiting for her to say.

"Dani." Bram returned his glass to the table and took her face in his hands because he wanted her nervously darting eyes on his. "You've known all along that I wanted you."

She swallowed. "Yes," she admitted in a ragged whisper. Her voice was shaky. Her world had turned shaky. "But that's all it is, Bram. Sex."

"Hell, I'm not some horny kid anymore, just looking to get laid. Besides, sex is easy. If all I wanted was a woman to share my bed, I didn't have to get married. All I'd have to do is pick up the phone.

"I'm in love with you, Mrs. Fortune. And these past days I've been going a little crazy because I don't know what the hell I'm going to do about it."

She wanted to believe that it was only the night and the moonlight talking. But she also knew that Bram, more than most, knew the difference between reality and illusion.

"I don't know what to say."

"How about telling me that I'm not completely crazy?" He took the mug from her trembling hand and deliberately placed it on the table beside his brandy snifter. "Tell me that I'm not imagining that you want me, too. Just a little?"

"More than a little," she whispered.

His lips brushed her temple. He lifted his gaze heavenward. "Thank you," he breathed. He ran his hand down her hair. Bram was feeling awkward and clumsy. No other woman had ever made him experience either reaction before.

"Tell me." His lips brushed hers, then retreated, before she could respond. Or reject. "Tell me again that you want me." He trailed his lips down her throat.

"I want you." Her breath trembled out. Her heart was beating like thunder in her head. "More than I ever thought possible." She moistened her lips as she felt a flutter that was both nervousness and excitement. "More than I should."

It wasn't exactly what he'd wanted to hear. But dammit, it was close enough. For now.

Because it had been too long, he kissed her then.

It was a long, lazy exploration of tastes that sent her head spinning. Her lips parted on a throaty moan as she poured herself into his kiss. A kiss that went on and on, deeper and deeper.

Her mouth was warm and willing, all traces of her earlier ambivalence swallowed up by the passion she'd tried so hard to deny. She linked her fingers together at the back of his head, molding his hot hungry mouth to hers.

Since no restraint was needed, Bram combed his hands through her hair, which was every bit as wild and unruly as her lovemaking had been that fateful night, months ago.

When he slipped his hands beneath the hem of her fleecy purple top, she stiffened. Then, as his fingers cupped her swelling breasts, she shuddered.

"You're so soft," he murmured wonderingly. He brushed his thumbs over her sensitized, lace-covered nipples. "The contrast never ceases to amaze me." His caressing touch had her pulse speeding. "The way your skin looks like porcelain." Although she knew such erotic thoughts were dangerous, Dani found herself wishing that he could touch her everywhere at once. "And feels like silk."

When his lips dampened the crimson lace, desire overruled reason. When he dispatched the front fastener of her bra with a practiced touch, giving his mouth access to her fragrant, powdered flesh, need overcame caution. As he leaned her back against the cushions, Dani clung to him mindlessly, willing to go anywhere he took her. His body was firm and strong and aroused against hers. But Dani experienced no fear.

She pressed hot, eager kisses over his face. She drew his bottom lip into the moist heat of her mouth and nibbled until his breath became as shallow and rapid as her own.

Her legs tangled with his. And when she shifted beneath him, arching her back, then moving in a slow, instinctive rhythmic motion, Bram had to grit his teeth to maintain control.

The swing began to rock wildly. Reminding himself that he hadn't planned on seducing her tonight—not while she was still harboring unresolved feelings for his brother—Bram forced himself, with herculean effort, to back away.

Because he wasn't quite ready to let her go, he gave her one last deep kiss that was part flare of passion, part glimmer of hope, part sigh of regret.

Then, depriving himself of her soft and fluid warmth, he reluctantly levered himself off her.

"Bram?" Her mind still fogged with desire, Dani looked up at him, openly confused.

"I'm sorry." He got up, walked to the end of the deck and stood there, his hands jammed into his back pockets as he stared out toward the sea. "That shouldn't have happened." He shook his head. "I never should have touched you. I never should have started something I wasn't about to finish."

Dani's heart was still pounding in her throat. Sitting up, she tried to refasten her bra. But her fingers had turned to stone, forcing her to abandon the task. She tugged the sweatshirt back down over her still-aching breasts.

"What if I wanted you to touch me?" she asked softly. "What if I wanted you to finish it?"

He turned back toward her and speared her with a clear, intent gaze. "Do you remember, the day of the funeral, when you called me selfish?"

She'd accused him of a lot of things that day, Dani remembered. Given the amount of liquor he'd consumed, she was surprised his memory was so clear.

"I seem to recall saying something like that, but I realize now that I was wrong."

"Actually, you were right." He came to stand in front of her. "I've recently discovered that I am a very selfish and greedy man, Dani. Enough so that I refuse to put up with three in a bed."

"I don't know what you're talking about." It was the first lie she'd told him since becoming his wife.

He bent down until they were eye to eye. "Then let me clarify it for you. When I make love to my wife, which, by the way, I have every intention of doing—hopefully sooner than later—I want to be certain that she knows exactly who it is who's kissing her." He rocked forward on the balls of his feet and brushed his lips against hers. Her moan merged with his.

"Who it is who's touching her." He cupped a dark hand over her unfettered breast. "And loving her."

He traced his tongue to her ear. "And when that day comes, my sweet wife, there will be no room for memories." He ran his hands down her body in slow, possessive strokes. "No place for ghosts." His teeth caught hold of her delicate lobe and tugged.

She was literally trembling. Although his touch was gentle and unthreatening, Dani felt as if an earthquake was taking place inside her body.

"I need time," she protested, even as she turned her head to recapture his roving lips. "To think."

"Fine."

It damn well wasn't his first choice. But Bram reminded himself that if he pushed Dani into consummating their marriage, nothing would be solved. Well, that wasn't entirely true. The ache in his groin would undoubtedly ease and he could give up the cold showers. But he was willing to put up with some temporary discomfort in order to win the lifetime prize.

He relinquished her sweet lips and sat down beside her.

"And while you're thinking," he suggested with an easy calm he was a hell of a long way from feeling, "why don't you tell me all about Dani Cantrell's life and times with that outwardly suave heir to all those petroleum millions, Peter Bannister IV?"

13

THE INTRUSION OF HER first, near-fatal marriage so abruptly after the blissfully passionate interlude, sent shock waves reverberating through Dani.

"Why on earth would you want to know about that?"

In reality, Dani had known, ever since the altercation in the gallery, that the subject would come up. She'd braced herself for it, even prepared a vague, noncommittal explanation about two mismatched people who'd mistakenly married in haste.

It was, after all, the truth. Not the whole truth, but enough.

But now, as she forced herself to meet her husband's steady gaze, she knew that Bram would never accept anything less than the entire ugly story.

"It has nothing to do with us," she insisted.

"Doesn't it? How about the little fact that whatever went wrong with Bannister is responsible for you believing that marriage is a dangerous and deadly trap?"

"That's not true." She paled at his gritty accusation. "In case you've forgotten, I was about to marry Ryan."

"There was no risk involved in that match." Bram's voice was clipped and hard. The need to know, to settle this problem once and for all, eclipsed his patience. "Ryan represented the known. The safe. My brother was like a protected harbor after a hurricane. Face it, Dani, you were using him."

It was not an easy thing for Bram to say. It had not been an easy thing for him to think.

At first, he'd feared that he was merely justifying his behavior, excusing having stolen his brother's fiancée. But the more he'd thought about it, the more Bram knew he was right.

"That's a horrid thing to say!" Dani jumped to her feet and glared down at him. Along with the expected anger, Bram detected a sudden tremor of desperation in her voice. "I loved Ryan!"

"I never said you didn't." He knew, without a shadow of a doubt, that Ryan and Dani had loved one another. Dearly. But it was, he considered, more like the love between a brother and a sister.

Bram knew there wasn't anything he could do to banish his brother from his wife's mind and heart. The undeniable truth was Ryan would always have a very special place in Dani's memories. He could, Bram had decided, live with that.

But the time had come to exorcise Bannister. Once and for all.

"You and Ryan probably would have had a good marriage," he allowed. "And if, after the first blush of newly wedded bliss wore off, there were days when you might think it a little too comfortable, if there were nights when you might secretly wish for a little more excitement, you probably would have kept your mouth shut and counted your many blessings.

"Unfortunately," he added, "we'll never really know what would have happened between you and Ryan. But I have a feeling a lot happened between you and Bannister. None of it pleasant."

"It wasn't exactly a picnic," she admitted. "But it's over. It's in the past." She swallowed the detestable taste of fear and fought the shame. "Can't we just leave it there?"

"I'd like to. But I can't." He automatically reached for a cigarette he no longer carried, then chose the brandy instead. "Not when whatever Bannister did to you has you afraid of me."

"But I'm not afraid of you, Bram."

"Aren't you?"

"Of course not." Of all the things she'd ever said to him, those words were the most truthful. Dani didn't add that what she feared was herself. Her feelings. "I know you'd never lift your hand to a woman."

"And Bannister did." It was not, Dani knew, a question.

Unable to accept the sympathy—or worse, the pity—she feared she'd see on his face, she turned away and stared out to sea. "Yes."

Her answer came as no surprise. What *was* a surprise was the flow of icy rage. Bram waited until he could speak calmly.

"What did he do to you?"

She shook her head. "It doesn't matter. Not anymore."

"What," Bram repeated quietly, insistently, "did Bannister do to you?"

"Why do you need to know? Can't you understand it's painful for me to talk about? Why would you want to hurt me this way?"

He forced himself not to succumb to the agony in her thready voice. "Sometimes the truth hurts. But sometimes it cleanses."

She whirled around to face Bram. "You want to know what he did?" Her eyes blazed with fury, her body trembled with pent-up rage. "Everything? Chapter and verse?"

"Everything," Bram said in a deceptively casual tone.

She stared down at him for a long, silent time. "All right." She pushed her shaking hands through her hair. "But this is the last time I'm ever going to talk about Peter Bannister again. After tonight, so far as our marriage is concerned, he doesn't exist."

That was precisely what Bram was counting on. "You've got yourself a deal."

Her shoulders lifted and dropped with a long exhaled breath. "Good." Because she could not relive those years and remain still, she began to pace.

"You have to understand," she began slowly, painfully, "when I first arrived in Paris, I had all these preconceived fantasies about becoming this bohemian artist, living in a garret, painting during the day and drinking wine in the cafés at night."

"With Matisse, Cézanne and Picasso."

"Yes." She managed a faint smile that Bram knew was directed inward. "I know it sounds ridiculously fanciful—"

"Not to anyone who spent a great deal of his youth making up imaginary conversations with Charlie Chaplin, John Ford and George Cukor."

His words had their desired effect. Her smile warmed ever so slightly. Their eyes met—hers pained, his encouraging. For an instant, Dani could almost believe that Bram, more than most, might actually be able to understand how she'd allowed her lifelong fantasies to get in the way of her better judgment.

She took a deep breath and began again. "When I first met Peter, he seemed like something out of an F. Scott Fitzgerald novel. He was witty and sophisticated and rich and just jaded enough to make him exciting."

"The Great Gatsby. Who, unfortunately turned out to be Tom Buchanan, Daisy's depraved husband." Remembering the barely suppressed violence in Bannister's eyes, Bram considered how closely he fit Fitzgerald's devastating profile of the brutality and moral carelessness of the idle rich.

"Exactly."

How strange it was, Dani mused, that Bram seemed to understand Peter's initial appeal so well, while Ryan, who'd loved her unequivocally, had never truly comprehended her reasons for entering into such a disastrous relationship.

Oh, her beloved childhood sweetheart had been unrelentingly sympathetic. And supportive. And to her eternal gratitude, he had never, ever, stopped loving her.

But the sad truth was that she'd never been able to make Ryan fully understand.

"We eloped to Monte Carlo the morning after we met. It seemed so glamorous. So exciting." She drew in a deep, shuddering breath and shook her head at the foolish young girl she'd once been. "I felt like a fairy-tale princess. For a few hours, at least. Until my wedding night."

Her voice, and her eyes, turned flat and distant. "Until Peter hit me."

Bram didn't speak. He didn't trust himself to speak. Or to move.

Dani was grateful when Bram didn't ask the obvious question. The question that young rookie policeman had asked her in the hospital. *Why did you stay?*

"I thought it was an aberration. He'd lost a lot of money at the casino, drunk a lot of champagne."

She began to pace again, eager to get the story finished. "I wanted to believe him when he said it would never happen again. I wanted—no, I needed—to believe I couldn't have made such a foolish error in judgment."

She sighed. "You know, I've always admired your parents. I think it's sweet how they're still in love after so many years. I love the way your father can still make your mother blush."

She turned back toward Bram. "Once, when I was about eleven, I saw them in the living room, slow dancing to the radio. That scene remains riveted in my mind as one of the most romantic moments I've ever witnessed. They were my ideal of what a perfect marriage should be."

"They had their fights," Bram felt obliged to say, remembering a few of the more colorful Donnybrooks. After all, his father could be as immovable as a rock. And his mother had inherited her own mother's Irish temper. Actually, now that he thought of it, Bram realized with some surprise, Dani reminded him a great deal of Amanda Fortune.

"I know they argued. And I realize they had their share of problems," Dani concurred. "But they stuck with each other, for better or worse, just the way the wedding vows said.

"I think that's why, in the beginning, I kept hoping I could make things right. Why I kept trying to make my marriage work. Because I didn't want to end up alone and divorced and bitter like my mother. I wanted to be happy and loved, like yours.

"We were living in San Francisco when things began to get really bad." She started to pace again. "Peter was spending all day at the office, then, instead of coming home, he'd go out with his friends. Sometimes he'd stay out all night."

"There were other women?"

"Yes." The shame had gone, Dani realized. And in its place was a pure and cleansing anger.

Bram couldn't imagine being married to Dani and craving any other female. "If the person I married was cheating on me, I'd be madder than hell."

"I should have been. But things were—" she paused, seeking the right word "—difficult. And when it finally sank in that the rumors about Peter's infidelity were true, I blamed myself."

"What the hell for?"

"For not satisfying him." Her voice was soft and hesitant, leading Bram to believe that even after all this time, there were still some scars that hadn't quite healed.

"You're kidding." Memories of their night together, never far from his mind, flooded back like a hot churning tide.

She moved her shoulders restlessly. "I wasn't as experienced as his other women. Or as sexually liberated. I didn't know what to do. What he wanted."

Lord, he'd done a number on her! How many ways, Bram wondered furiously, had Bannister found to humiliate his wife?

Wishing he'd just killed the guy while he'd had a chance, and impatient with Dani for continuing, in this last way, to let the bastard play with her mind, Bram refilled his brandy glass to keep himself from shaking her.

"Did it ever occur to you," he asked in an even, clipped voice, "that Bannister was to blame for any problems you and he may have had in the bedroom?"

"But all those women... So many different women..."
Dani bit her lip and looked away.

Bram's curse was low and vicious. "Believe me, Dani, so long as you don't look like the hunchback of Notre-Dame and have a few bucks in your pocket, it doesn't take much to coax a different faceless female to bed every night.

"Actually, it's pretty much a cinch. All you have to do is concern yourself with what you want. Your needs. Your desires. And if you haven't satisfied the woman, no big deal. Because tomorrow night there will be another one. And another.

"Until one day you've lost track, which doesn't really matter, since you never really cared about any of them anyway."

Dani felt a prick of jealousy at the way Bram sounded as if he was more than a little familiar with such behavior.

"If you're trying to convince me that all men—"

"Dammit, that's not what I'm talking about!" Bram roared, his own anger finally getting the better of him. "I'm talking about making a commitment to one special woman. To caring about her needs. Her desires. I'm talking about wanting to make her happy. Every night of both your lives."

"Oh." A little chastised, she tried a faint smile that failed miserably. "I'm sorry."

"Hell." Like everything else about Dani, this discussion wasn't going at all according to plan. He'd vowed to himself to refrain from judging her. He'd sworn to withhold criticism.

"I don't want you to apologize, Dani. I just want you to understand that I'm not Bannister."

"I know that."

It was, Bram told himself, a start. "And by the way, sweetheart, if you'd been any hotter that night we spent together, we would have burned the cabin down."

As she felt color flood into her cheeks, Dani was relieved that it was too dark for Bram to see her blush.

"Thank you," she murmured.

"Don't thank me for telling the truth."

The night was growing cooler. Bram observed Dani's slight shiver. "Maybe we should go inside," he suggested.

"No." Dani preferred telling her sordid little tale outside, in the open air, where the night shadows could conceal her face and the sea breeze could blow her words away. "I'd rather stay out here."

"Then come sit down beside me." He held out his hand. "And let me keep you warm."

And safe. The words, unspoken but crystal clear, hovered between them.

The lure was too strong. Too inviting. Dani returned to the swing. Eager to finally put these last painful vestiges of the past behind her, she leaned her head against Bram's shoulder, closed her eyes and told him everything.

It was as if a dam had burst. The words flooded out, sometimes tumbling over one another. She revealed her former husband's chronic infidelity, the continual mental abuse that bordered on psychological terrorism. She confessed to living with constant dread and fear—dread that she would wake up each morning, and fear, during that final beating, that she might not.

Bram remained quiet as Dani talked. And talked. And talked. A strong offshore wind blew away the clouds, revealing a bright circle of light around a full white moon. And still the horrifying words continued to pour from her.

Finally, she ran down, having nothing left to say, nor the energy to say it.

Bram sat there, stroking her hair, trying to control the rage that had been building in him. He'd always known that the world was a cruel and often-vicious place. He made a living probing beneath the pretty surfaces of relationships, prying into intimate secrets, ripping the scabs off emotional sores. *Scandals* was only the most recent in a long line. And all the time he'd managed to remain removed from his stories.

He'd thought that there was nothing that could shock him. No behavior cruel or mean enough to shake him.

He'd thought wrong.

He'd wanted to know everything about Dani's marriage to Peter Bannister. He'd demanded she tell him every sordid detail.

And now that he knew the hell she'd survived, Bram felt raw inside.

He closed his eyes and forced himself to remain where he was when what he wanted to do was track Bannister down like the animal he was and murder him.

"You've no idea," he said in a low, rough voice, "how much I admire you."

Exhausted and drained, Dani looked up at him. "Why?"

"For being who you are." He smoothed her hair away from her face and brushed a soft kiss against her temple. "What you are."

Emotion coursed through him. He ran a soothing palm down her hair and realized that his own hands were none too steady.

"I promise you, Dani. He'll never hurt you again." He framed her face in his hands. "No one will ever hurt you again."

And as she looked into his still-angry dark eyes, Dani trusted. And believed.

As Bram had hoped, the intensely emotional conversation created an important shift in their relationship. Most important, there was no more talk of an annulment. And while he was not certain whether that was because she'd truly decided to give their marriage a chance, or had simply decided to abide by their original agreement to wait until after the baby was born, Bram was grateful for the change.

They began eating breakfast together each morning, dinner together at night, after which they would stroll hand in hand along the beach. During these interludes, as all lovers do when getting to know one another, they talked of everything. And nothing. The important thing was that they were together. And that they were talking.

Bram was admittedly disappointed and frustrated when Dani didn't move from the guest room across the hall to his bed, but, reminding himself that patience was a virtue, he waited. And continued to court his wife.

Which was, he realized one afternoon as he'd stopped by a florist for a bouquet of daisies, exactly what he was doing. Bram was not all that familiar with the formal courtship ritual. After all, the women in the world where he lived and worked had always known the score. Forthright, outspoken and liberated, they were just as apt to suggest having sex as he was. And when the relationship ended, as it always did, they were just as quick to move on to other men. Other beds.

But Dani was different. His feelings for her were different. She was, quite simply, worth the extra effort. Having rushed her into marriage, Bram now felt the responsibility to make the time to properly woo his bride.

For her part, Dani was amazed at how well they were getting along. And, even more amazingly, how much they had in common.

Both she and Bram believed *Vertigo* to be a Hitchcock masterpiece and Kim Novak's best work. Both considered *Double Fantasy* John Lennon's most innovative work, even though they continued to believe that Yoko Ono was more than a little responsible for the Beatles' breakup.

Along with similar tastes in movies and music, they read the same books, although they did disagree vehemently concerning a recent runaway bestseller. It came as a surprise to Dani—who'd learned the hard way not to question her first husband's judgment about anything—that she and Bram could argue so heatedly without having the disagreement flow over into any other portion of their lives. Indeed, after they'd finally agreed to disagree, Bram had floored her by agreeing to give the novel a second read.

Both enjoyed ethnic restaurants, long weekends and Sunday-morning crossword puzzles, though Bram drove Dani slightly crazy by insisting on doing his portion in ink. Both shared a distaste for small dogs, reckless rollerbladers who ran you off the ocean walk, and unauthorized biographies.

And most important, on a list from one to ten, both Bram and Dani ranked family first.

During their time together, Bram came to realize that his wife was neither as flighty nor as self-centered as he'd always thought her to be.

While Dani discovered her husband to be far more serious and much more caring than what his often cynical, brash demeanor projected to the outside world.

One morning, nearly a month after Bram's return from Thailand, Dani pulled out a photo of Ryan from the drawer of the guest-room nightstand. The candid snapshot had been taken during a rare sunny winter day at Golden Gate Park. She remembered how they'd been so much in love that day, laughing together in the benevolent sunshine. Two weeks later, he was gone.

The mattress sighed as she sat down on the edge of the bed. "Bram and I are married now, Ryan," she said softly. "And I'm pregnant. But I suppose you know that."

A sob caught in her throat, blocking off her words. She squeezed her eyes shut, fighting back tears. "You always were my rock," she whispered falteringly. "And I m-miss you so much."

Drawing in a deep breath, she opened her eyes again and ran her fingers caressingly over his handsome, smiling face.

"At first I felt guilty about making love to Bram. But now I really can't, anymore. Because of the baby. Our baby. Bram's and mine."

She placed her palms against her gently rounded stomach. "I love this baby already, Ryan. So very, very much. More than anything. And there's something else."

The warm blue eyes she remembered so well appeared soothingly encouraging. Allowing her to say, for the first time, the thought that had been in her mind for days. Weeks.

"I love Bram, too." It didn't seem strange to Dani that she would admit these feelings to Ryan before she revealed them to her husband.

All her life, Ryan had been her sounding board. And while his death had changed so many things in Dani's life, she realized that this, at least for now, remained exactly the same. "I didn't mean to fall in love with him. And if you'd lived, it never would have happened.

"But now it has. And Bram says he loves me, and although I found it hard to accept when he first told me—you remember how we used to go out of our way to ignore each other—now I believe him. After all, we both know Bram doesn't ever say anything he doesn't mean."

Her faltering voice grew stronger.

"I know Bram and I can make our marriage work. I believe we can make each other—and our children—happy."

Dani rose slowly. She stood there, looking down at the photo, for a long, silent time.

Finally, with a whispered "Goodbye, dear," she placed the photo in a wooden box tucked away in the back of the closet. Inside the box was a gilt-lettered wedding invitation and the sketch pad filled with Ryan's smiling image.

She tenderly laid the snapshot beside the smaller blue velvet box containing Ryan's engagement ring.

Knowing Ryan would want her to get on with her life, secure in the knowledge that all he'd ever wanted for her was that she be happy, Dani shut the lid of the teak box, effectively closing a very special chapter in her life.

Then, wiping away the single tear that had trailed silently down her cheek, she went downstairs to have breakfast with her husband.

14

"SO," BRAM SAID twenty minutes later, smiling at her across the table, "today's the big day."

Dani had been volunteering at the shelter three days a week for the past month and already she'd discovered a mother lode of talent. While the residents might not possess a great deal of technical skills, the emotion they poured onto their canvases was riveting. So much so, she was going to broach the idea of a fund-raising art show to Madeline Hartlove this afternoon.

She ran her finger around the rim of her cup. "I just hope Madeline likes the idea."

"She'll love it because it answers so many needs. Number one, it'll help boost the women's self-esteem, number two—" he ticked the reasons off on his fingers "—it'll raise funds, and three, it'll garner publicity, which will bring in more money."

"And get the word out to more women who need help."

"Exactly." Their eyes met in an unspoken acknowledgment of the fact that she'd once been in that number. Not wanting to darken the mood, Bram plucked a plump ripe strawberry from the bowl between them and held it out to her. Seeing through his ploy to change the subject and keep her from dwelling on the past, she smiled and took a bite of the berry.

The gesture, like so many things Dani did, was unconsciously erotic. Bram felt the painful ache of desire and wondered how much longer he could refrain from making love to his wife.

"I knew I'd have you eating out of my hand one of these days." His voice was roughened, but his teasing smile kept her from taking his male arrogance seriously.

"What's sauce for the goose . . ." she murmured silkily, selecting another scarlet berry from the silver bowl.

She gazed at him through a thick veil of sooty lashes. Her lips curved in sensual invitation and her sultry expression, as she held the strawberry inches from his mouth, suggested that a great deal more than fruit was being offered.

Playing the game, Bram took a big, bold bite. When his teeth brushed against her fingertips, Dani felt a corresponding shock of sexual desire shimmy all the way through her.

It was certainly not the first time the chemistry that had erupted full-blown between them that fateful night had flared during their weeks of living together. It was, however, the first time that Dani couldn't think of a single reason to deny what she'd secretly been wanting to do since they'd stood out on the tarmac in that electrically charged desert night after their marriage.

It was as if by finally saying goodbye to Ryan, she'd freed herself to make love with her husband. When she would have taken her hand away, he caught hold of it and began nibbling seductively at her fingertips. "What time are you due at the shelter?"

His touch, the look he was giving her over their joined hands, was making her melt. "I'm usually there by nine-thirty."

A half hour, Bram considered, wouldn't begin to be enough time. After all, he'd waited for weeks. Now he fully intended to do this right.

"But," Dani suggested breathlessly, as his tongue gathered in the sweet strawberry juice from her flesh, "I could be late."

Desire flared, hot and wicked in his midnight blue eyes. Bram was about to take her up on her gilt-edged feminine invitation, when the phone rang.

"We'll let the recorder get it." He rose from the table, drawing her up to stand in the circle of his arms.

The way she was looking up at him, her warm and loving heart shining in her eyes, made Bram feel like the richest man alive.

They stood there, basking in the warmth of a buttery yellow sunbeam, both wanting to draw the exquisite moment out.

In the distance, they were vaguely aware of Bram's voice on the machine, instructing the caller to leave a message.

"Hello, Bram? This is Hugh. If you're there, pick up, dammit," the obviously stressed male voice demanded. "We've got a problem. There was a fire in your office last night."

Those words garnered both Bram's and Dani's unwilling but immediate attention. They looked over at the machine, as if envisioning Hugh Wingate, Bram's assistant. "The fire department arrived in time to keep it from being a total loss, but I gotta tell you, it's not pretty. The fire investigator's due here any time. He wants to talk to you."

Bram's curse was short and pungent.

"You'd better go." Dani placed her palm against the side of his face and felt his muscles tense.

"Hell." *Timing*, Bram reminded himself, *was everything*.

"It's just as well," Dani said, sounding as disappointed as he was angry. "I really do need to talk with Madeline before today's lesson."

Go. Stay. The two words warred in his mind. Having always considered himself a man of quick and firm decisions, such vacillation was both uncharacteristic and unwanted.

"I've got an idea," he said, struggling for a workable compromise. "It's obvious that I'm not going to get any work done today." He drew her closer. "So, why don't you drop by the studio after your lesson? We can drive up to Santa Barbara and have lunch in that new Indian place everyone's raving about."

"Lunch sounds perfect." Tilting her head, Dani twined her arms around Bram's neck. "But why don't we have a picnic instead?" She went up on her toes and lifted her lips to his.

"A picnic?" Her mouth was every bit as warm as he remembered. Its taste even more potent. "On the beach?"

"The beach is always nice." Her lips curved against his, her smile dazzling, irresistible. Her rounded, intensely female body molded perfectly against his. "But a bit predictable, don't you think?"

"Predictable?" he asked numbly, as hunger coursed through him. As she slowly traced the shape of his bottom lip with her tongue, it crossed Bram's mind that he was being thoroughly, expertly seduced.

"I was thinking—" she reached up, brushed his dark hair from his forehead, then watched it fall back into place "—that anyone can have breakfast in bed." She tugged his shirt free of his jeans, her hands teasing, tempting, as they roamed across his back. "But now, lunch in bed . . ."

With a muffled sound that was part groan, part oath, Bram lowered his head and captured her mouth.

Passion, too long denied, flared until it threatened to consume. Minds emptied. Tastes tangled. Hearts entwined.

And then, too soon for either of them, the fiery kiss ended. Bram reluctantly put her a little away from him, his breath raw and ragged. Dani drew in a steadying breath, but could manage only a shallow, shaky one.

Lord, she was beautiful, Bram thought, looking down into her exquisite, love-softened face. And she was his.

Despite whatever smoldering mess might be waiting for him at Eclipse Studios, Bram was feeling on top of the world.

He grinned and pressed his fingers against her still-tingling lips. "Keep that thought. For later."

Her warm answering grin reached her eyes. "Later."

DANI WAS PLEASED when all the women wanted to participate in the art project to show they were on the road to recovery.

"Speaking of recovery," Georgia O'Hara said, "I got accepted to that program I applied to. I start next week."

"That's wonderful!" Dani hugged her. She knew that Georgia, who'd worked as a registered nurse, had almost given up hope of getting into the nurse-practitioner school. "You must be excited."

"I am. So's Brian."

Dani's blood chilled. "You called him?"

"He's my husband," Georgia reminded Dani gently.

"You didn't tell him where you were?"

"It may have come up," Georgia admitted. "He's been so worried, not knowing where I was."

Alarms were going off inside Dani. "But Georgia—"

"It's all right. I just wanted Bri to realize that things were going to get better."

She was so happy. Though she wanted to warn Georgia not to trust so easily, Dani could not bring herself to take the woman's newfound hope away.

She hugged Georgia again. "I hope everything works out for you."

An hour later, Brian O'Hara showed up at the Anchorage. Although it was not yet noon, he was already drunk.

And he was armed.

THE PICKETERS WERE BACK, marching in front of the studio, chanting their doggerel. From the number of signs predicting that he'd be the next to burn—in hell—Bram realized that word of the fire had already gotten out.

His office was nearly gutted. The white walls were blackened with smoke; the glass fronting the antique movie posters had shattered and the aluminum frames had twisted from the intense heat.

"It's not as bad as it looks," the fire investigator assured him.

Rather than the navy T-shirt usually worn by a fireman, he was wearing a navy suit. Tall and lean, darkly tanned with well-trimmed silver hair, he could, Bram mused, his director's mind always working, get work as a double for Paul Newman.

"You were lucky. Whoever set it was definitely an amateur."

His casual tone garnered Bram's immediate attention. "Set it?" He glanced over at Hugh, who shrugged in response. "Are you saying this is arson?"

"We found two bottles of white gas, attached to electric timers. The one in this room went off, the one in the john didn't."

"Arson," Bram repeated numbly.

"Arson," the investigator agreed. "So, Mr. Fortune, the question of the day is, who hates you enough to do this?"

Two hours later, Bram had been grilled on every aspect of his life—personal and work. He felt as if he'd just undergone the third degree, which made him wonder, if fire investigators were so hard on the victims, how the hell did they treat the arsonists?

"So, our only lead is that group picketing outside the studio," the investigator said.

"I can't think of anyone else. I'm in a highly competitive profession. Sure, I've probably made a few enemies along the way, but we tend to attack each other in the trade papers. Not with gasoline and electric timers."

The Paul Newman look-alike glanced up from his notepad. "Speaking of newspapers—"

Bram knew what was coming. "My wife's ex-husband has nothing to do with this."

"I read he made threats." When Bram gave him a long, censorious stare, a dark flush rose from the investigator's starched white collar. "It was hard to miss," he defended himself. "I stopped by Ralph's to pick up some coffee and a six-pack and there it was, right by the register."

"There's more fiction in one issue of that rag than in all the scripts produced in this town in a year." Bram's voice was rough and gritty.

"I suppose that's true." The investigator made another note. "But I'll still want to talk to your wife."

"Is that really necessary?" Bram knew how difficult it had been for Dani to discuss Bannister with him. He wanted to protect her from having to air her dirty laundry to a stranger.

"I'm afraid it is, Mr. Fortune."

"Hell." Bram plowed his hands through his hair. "All right," he agreed reluctantly. "But I want to be there when you talk with her."

"I don't have any problem with that."

"When?"

"No time like the present," the investigator replied. "The sooner we can cross her ex off the suspect list, the sooner we can find who it is that doesn't like you." He returned his silver pen to his shirt pocket.

"She's not home right now," Bram said. "Why don't I pick her up at the shelter where she's working and bring her to the house? You can meet us there."

"Whatever works for you," the older man said obligingly.

Bram was driving to the shelter, the radio tuned to a local news station, when a sudden bulletin made his heart lurch.

There had been a shooting, the reporter informed the listening audience. At a women's shelter called the Anchorage.

Although details were sketchy, and the police had yet to issue a report, neighbors were telling reporters on the scene that two women had been taken to the hospital by ambulance.

Bram was about to call the shelter on his cellular phone when the reporter's next words had him making an illegal U-turn.

According to an unnamed source at the hospital, one of the women currently being treated in the emergency room was the pregnant wife of Hollywood director Bram Fortune.

15

PRAYERS HE THOUGHT he'd forgotten reverberated through Bram's mind as he pulled the Jaguar up in front of the double glass doors with a screech of brakes. He ignored the No Parking sign; let them tow the damn car.

The air in the emergency-room waiting area was rife with the scents of disinfectant, pain, fear and despair. Every chair was claimed, forcing dozens of patients to stand.

"Where is she?" he demanded of the clerk on duty. He had to shout to be heard over the sudden blare of the code horn and a robotic voice instructing the trauma team to report to the ER. "Where's my wife?"

The elderly woman—whose badge pinned to the pink and white smock pronounced her to be a volunteer—stopped charting long enough to look up over the half lenses of her reading glasses.

"Your wife?"

"Dani—Danielle Fortune."

"Fortune?" Her tone suggested unfamiliarity with the name. "Did we notify you, Mr. Fortuno?"

"Fortune," Bram grated from between clenched teeth. "The name is Bramwell Fortune. And my wife's name is Danielle Fortune. I heard on my car radio that she was brought here after a shooting at the Anchorage battered-women's shelter.

"Ah." The clerk nodded. She began leafing through a stack of pink, yellow and white forms. "The gunshot victim."

Those three words were all it took for Bram's already unsteady heart to plummet to his feet. "Dani was shot?" He could feel the blood draining from his face. "Where is she, dammit?" He pounded his fist on the counter.

"Please, Mr. Fortuno," she sniffed, "if you'll remain calm, I'll attempt to find out." She turned to a computer, her fingers moving laboriously over the keyboard. "I don't see her listed, but if she just came in . . ." More keyboard tapping.

Bram watched the screen change. "Ah, here she is." *Tap-tap-tap.* "Yes. She was taken upstairs. To surgery."

Bram had thought he couldn't feel any more panicky. He'd thought wrong. "Dani's in surgery?"

He'd never experienced such a paralyzing depth of fear. Not during the avalanche, not even when he'd watched Ryan being carried away by those rumbling, murderous snows.

If anything happened to Dani . . .

No! Bram shook his head, refusing to even think it.

"Excuse me," a female voice said behind him. "Mr. Fortune?"

He spun around and found himself looking down into the owlish gaze of a young woman. Her blond hair had been tied back in a tidy twist at the nape of her neck. Her eyes behind the tortoiseshell-framed lenses were as blue green as a tropical lagoon and every bit as calm. Which was a decided contrast to the blood spattered over her green scrubs and white shoes.

Oh, God. Was that Dani's blood? Bram wondered with horror.

"I'm Bram Fortune."

"I'm Dr. Nelson. I treated your wife when she came in."

The doors slid open with a rush of air. Paramedics hurried in, pushing a gurney on which a teenager with a severe scalp laceration had been strapped down. One of the paramedics was shouting out vital signs to the waiting team.

Obviously accustomed to working amid such pandemonium, Dr. Nelson deftly moved aside as the patient and the team rushed past on their way into the adjoining trauma treatment room.

"Your wife is going to be fine," she continued. "Your baby, as well."

Relief flooded over him. Bram felt his knees trying to buckle and concentrated on standing upright and not humiliating himself by passing out. "The clerk said she was in surgery."

"*Mrs. O'Hara* was taken into surgery," she corrected with a sharp look at the clerk who shrugged and returned to her paperwork. "I'm afraid her condition is serious. She was shot several times."

"Was Dani shot, too?"

"No. Your wife suffered some cuts from flying glass, which we've cleaned. Only one required stitches. Apparently the gunman sprayed a great many bullets around the room. One of those shots shattered a mirror."

The last of Bram's fear was burned away by the very real rage that after having escaped her own abusive situation, Dani could have been killed by another brutal husband.

"What happened to O'Hara?" Hanging was too good for the man who'd harmed his wife, Bram decided.

"I'm sorry, but I can't divulge—"

"Look, Doctor," Bram interrupted, "I'm not going to call a press conference and announce it to the world. I just want to be able to tell my wife she doesn't have to worry about the guy coming after her again any time soon."

"No. She doesn't have to worry about that," Dr. Nelson confirmed. "According to the paramedics, Mr. O'Hara shot himself after believing he'd killed his wife. He was DOA."

"I want to see my wife."

"Of course." The doctor smiled. "I'm sure she's anxious to see you, as well." She gestured toward a set of swing doors. "She's through there, in the third treatment room on the right."

"Thank you, Doctor." Although tempted, he refrained from kissing her.

Dani was sitting on the edge of the metal table when Bram entered the treatment room. A white butterfly tape marred her cheek, another had been placed at her right temple. Above her left eyebrow was a row of unsightly stitches. For a fleeting moment, all his fury and earlier feelings of impotence centered on the bruise forming around the dark sutures.

Warmth flooded into her eyes when she saw him. "Oh, Bram." She slid off the table and into his arms.

"It's all right," he soothed, stroking her hair, holding her close and thanking God, or the stars, or whatever other fates had kept his wife safe from harm. "He can't hurt you anymore."

His touch was so heartbreakingly gentle. Dani remembered a time when she'd believed Bram to be a man incapable of gentleness. As she wrapped her arms around him and hung on tight, Dani realized how wrong she'd been.

"I could have lost you." His voice was as raw and rough as his still-ragged emotions.

"Never." Her eyes misted at the love she heard in Bram's tone. "You're stuck with me, remember? For better or worse."

"Forever."

"Did the doctor tell you anything about Georgia?"

"She's in surgery. It's touch and go."

"Oh, God."

Dani closed her eyes, which proved a mistake as the terrifying scene at the shelter replayed in her mind. She rested her forehead against Bram's shoulder. It was a strong shoulder. A comforting one. Dani felt at home there.

"Hold me." She only needed a moment, she assured herself, hating her weakness, accepting his strength. Just a brief moment to pull herself together again.

"As long as you want."

They stood that way for a long, silent time. There was no passion. No fire. Just comfort. And love.

Her trembling subsided. Her flesh began to warm. Her heart, which he could feel beating against his, gradually calmed.

"Did the doctor tell you what happened to Brian?" Her words were muffled by his shirt. "I saw him shoot himself, but—"

"He's dead."

Dani sighed. "That's so sad."

"Better him than you." Rage simmered in Bram again. A hot fury he struggled, for Dani's sake, to tamp down. His hands tangled in her hair as he tilted her head back and looked down into her pale face. "If he'd hurt you, or the baby—"

It was her turn to soothe him. "He didn't." She pressed her lips against his and tasted his anger. And his fear.

She tasted so sweet. Even sweeter than her murmured sigh. Bram discovered that it was impossible to remain angry while kissing this woman.

Dani felt the change in him as his lips softened and plucked at hers, teasing, tasting, tempting. With an inarticulate murmur, she twined her arms around his neck and parted her lips, opening, offering.

Her heartbeat began to accelerate again—with passion this time, rather than pain. Needs tangled sinuously with nerves, pleasure vibrated through her.

He cupped his hand behind her neck. "Let's go home."

Dani couldn't think of anything she'd rather do. It was what she wanted. What she needed. But—

"I can't. Not until Georgia's out of surgery."

He understood her concern. But right now his concern was centered on his wife and unborn child. "That could be hours. You've had a terrifying day. You need your rest."

"I'll rest later. After Georgia's out of danger."

He'd come to know Dani well enough to realize when he'd run into the brick wall of her intransigence. "Let me talk to

Dr. Nelson," he suggested. "If we're staying, I want you to have a room where you can lie down."

"You're going to spoil me." A soft smile took the complaint from her tone.

"I'm going to do my damnedest," he promised.

The hours dragged on. Her nerves on edge, Dani had yearned to pace the corridor, but Dr. Nelson—who'd rounded up an empty room—had agreed with Bram that Dani should try to relax. If not for herself, for her child, who'd received quite an adrenaline rush today. That was all it took for Dani to give in to Bram's demand that she sit down.

They tried to carry on a normal conversation. Bram told her about the fire, belatedly remembering to call the investigator's pager and inform him that he was going to have to wait until tomorrow to interview Dani.

He went down to the cafeteria and brought them both back a lunch neither really wanted. And still they waited.

Finally, just when Dani didn't think she could take it anymore, a dark-haired, middle-aged man clad in blue scrubs and booties, with his blue mask around his neck, entered the room.

"Mrs. Fortune?"

"That's me." Dani's heart was in her throat.

"I'm Dr. Dalgleish. Your friend is going to be fine."

Relief was instantaneous. "Can I see her?"

"She's in post-op right now. It would be better if you wait until tomorrow. She wouldn't remember you were here," he added, anticipating her planned argument.

"If you're sure." She exchanged a worried look with Bram.

"We'll call every few hours," he suggested. "If her condition changes—"

"Which we don't expect," Dr. Dalgleish put in.

"We'll come back," Bram promised.

It was, she supposed, the best solution. After thanking the doctor, Dani went home with Bram in a cab. The Jag had been towed.

Dani was relieved when Bram didn't seem to expect conversation. She remained quiet, lost in her own thoughts. It was only when she was safely in the beach house that she allowed her tautly held emotions to break free.

He stayed behind to pay the driver. When he entered the house, Bram found her standing at the window, her arms tightly wrapped around herself, her head lowered, weeping.

Without a word, he picked her up and carried her upstairs to his bed and sat down beside her, drawing her close.

She curled against him like a kitten seeking comfort from a raging storm as she continued to sob against his shoulder. The sun was setting into the sea when the trembling finally ceased.

"I'm sorry." Her tears had stopped, but her breathing still came in hitches.

"Don't." He brushed her tumbled hair back from her face and kissed her wet cheek. "Don't ever apologize for being human."

"I hate weakness." Her hands balled into fists against his chest. His shirt was soaked through.

"It's not weakness to be scared when a madman's pointing a gun at you." An errant tear slid slowly down her cheek. Bram tenderly brushed it away with his knuckle. "It's not weakness to be shaken when that same man shoots up the place, then violently takes his own life right in front of you."

He traced her still-trembling lips with a fingertip. "And it's definitely not weakness to be relieved that you didn't die."

"I knew he wasn't going to kill me," Dani said raggedly.

"You were that sure of him?"

"Not of him. Of us." She managed a watery smile. "I firmly believe we're destined to spend our old age in matching rockers out on the deck, watching our great-grandchildren building sand castles and frolicking in the surf."

Just as Dani was the woman Bram had always needed, without knowing he was needy, the image her words invoked was exactly what he'd always wanted, without having realized he'd been wanting.

Their eyes touched. And then their hearts.

And Dani knew it was time.

"I smell like disinfectant," she complained, wrinkling her nose.

"You smell like paradise. But I'll run a bath."

"I'd rather have a shower." She needed to stand under a purifying hot spray, she needed to scrub away any lingering vestiges of Brian O'Hara. "And then I want you to make love with me."

"Dani..." It was what he wanted, as well. And at any other time, Bram would have given everything he owned to hear those long-awaited words from her. But he'd taken advantage of her vulnerability once before.

"I know what I'm asking, Bram," she said softly. Insistently. "I know what I want." She ran her fingertips down the side of his face, around his rigid jaw. "And I want my husband."

He still had his doubts. But as her stroking touch made his blood burn, Bram reminded himself that it had been Ryan, not he, who'd been the saint in the Fortune family.

"Sweetheart, I thought you'd never ask." Bram turned on the water in the shower, then undressed her slowly, his fingers flicking open the buttons running down the front of her blouse. He frowned at the blood spatters on the emerald silk and once again was forced to restrain his fury.

Dani saw his lips draw into a tight line. "Bram?"

"Sorry." He shook off the lingering anger. "I was just thinking—" he slipped the loosened blouse off one shoulder "—about how much I love you—" then the other. "Every time I look at you, every time I kiss you, I fall in love all over again."

She smiled at that. A feminine smile shimmering with sensual intent. "Then don't stop looking." Her dark eyes tempted, her luscious lips lured. "Don't stop kissing."

He rocked forward and brushed his lips against hers. "I don't intend to." He buried his mouth in her throat and imagined he could taste the heated beat of her blood. "Ever."

He drew the blouse down her arms, then tossed it carelessly into the wastebasket.

"Bram," she complained weakly, as his mouth returned to hers again and lingered. Eager now, she began tugging on the buttons of his shirt. "That blouse is brand-new."

"It's stained. I'll buy you a new one." He wanted no memories of this morning's horror left behind. "I'll buy you a dozen. A hundred new blouses."

She laughed a little breathlessly as his palm brushed over her swelling breast. "Oh, I do like having a rich husband."

"Whatever you want," he promised. Her bra followed the blouse. Her breasts were fuller. Entranced, he traced a faint blue vein from crest to straining nipple with a fingertip, delighting in the way his caress could make her tremble. "You name it." His hands glided over her flesh with exquisite patience, like whispers on silk, creating heat wherever they touched. "And it's yours."

Steam rose, surrounding them in a mist as warm as that surrounding her mind. Dani folded his shirt back and pressed her lips against his bare chest. "You," she whispered.

The tip of her tongue trailed wetly down the axis of his body and from the way he shuddered, from the way his stomach muscles quivered as her tongue glided over them, Dani knew that Bram was every bit as seduced as she. "I want you."

The breath was clogging in his lungs. When her hands began to unfasten his slacks, Bram felt the desperate control he'd been attempting to maintain threaten to slip away.

"Later." He captured her open mouth again with a deep, wet kiss. His fingers circled the rosy nipples of her breasts, drawing a soft moan of surrender. "Soon."

Although it took a mighty effort, Bram managed to undress Dani without dragging her to the floor and burying himself in her silken warmth. His own clothes he practically ripped away.

The torment was exquisite, the pleasure sublime. Dani felt her bones liquefying even before Bram drew her under the hot spray.

She'd used Bram's hedonistic shower before, but never had the four pulsating jets felt so erotic. The spray hit her skin like a thousand vibrating fingers, front and back—against her shoulders, her breasts, her back, her bottom—creating needles of pleasure-pain against flesh that his fingers had already sensitized beyond belief.

The water streamed over them. The heat lamp overhead cast a ruby glow over their wet bodies. They were engulfed in clouds of steam.

Bram picked up the bar of soap, rubbed it between his palms to create a lather, then began running it over her slick wet body, spreading the fragrant bubbles like a luminous cape and reveling in the shuddering, gasping sounds of her breathing that signaled her own loss of control.

He lingered at her heavy breasts until they were achingly full with pleasure. His hands were rough at the palms but silky smooth with soap; the sensual combination took her deeper and deeper, until she was drunk and dazed with pleasure.

And then down, slowly, erotically, lower and lower, while her fingers clenched and unclenched in his hair. The feel of his hands splayed across her stomach made her moan. The nip of his teeth against the wet flesh at her inner thigh created a jolt of heat.

Dani's body craved. Her heart hungered. She reached for him, but groggily, as if in a dream. Evading her touch, Bram continued his erotic journey, drawing out the sensations until her head was spinning from need.

"Bram . . ." Water was streaming over her, over him. She was drowning in emotions. Desperation rose. "Please."

His lips were creating havoc at her ankle. When the desperate plea shuddered from her parted lips, his mouth roved slowly back up her quivering legs.

Her body arched up as his mouth found her. Stunned by the jolt of heat, Dani cried out in astonished pleasure. Dizzy, she clutched at his shoulders. Before she could recover, Bram's tongue speared inside her, giving her another hot, quick orgasm that rocked her to the core and left her trembling.

She went limp; Bram held her, not allowing her to fall as she lost herself to the spiraling pleasure. "Lord, you're wonderful," he murmured, his rough voice revealing his own hunger. His mouth found hers again and drank deeply. "I can't believe you're mine."

"Yours," she whispered against his wicked, wonderful lips. She'd never known it could be like this. She'd never known *she* could be like this. "For eternity."

"For eternity." With his hands still on her hips, he lifted her up, joining their bodies, hot slick flesh to hot slick flesh.

Over the fevered beat of blood pounding in her head, Dani heard him say her name. It sounded wonderful. He murmured delicious promises, swore lavish vows. And she believed him. Totally.

16

ONCE THE LAST EMOTIONAL barricades came down, Bram and Dani felt like giddy, love-struck newlyweds. As the weeks went by, they basked in each other's company. They laughed. And loved. And together they reveled in the miraculous changes taking place in Dani's body.

Of course, they still argued. They were both, after all, stubborn, independent, creative people. But their fights were like shooting stars—hot, fast, and quickly gone. Besides, Bram had discovered, there was a lot to be said for making up.

His wife and his child meant everything to him. So much so, that Bram couldn't even concern himself when the fire investigator could prove no link between any of the protesting groups and the suspected arson at the studio.

He didn't even mind when he discovered that the contents of his office—including his beloved posters—had been underinsured. He could lose everything he owned, and still be a wealthy man. Because he had Dani. And their baby.

"Oh, my God," she gasped one morning. She was still lying in bed, luxuriating in the warm afterglow of their lovemaking, while Bram dressed for work.

"What's the matter?" Concerned, he spun around. When he saw her clutching at her belly, Bram's heart clenched. "Dani? Is anything wrong? Is it the baby?"

She couldn't be in labor. It was only the middle of June; the baby wasn't due until November.

"No." Her eyes were as wide as saucers. "Yes."

"Which is it, dammit?" Panic created impatience. He tried to remember what he'd read about premature infants, feared this would be too early for survival. "Yes? Or no?"

"Both." Bram was sitting beside her on the bed now, his handsome face ashen with husbandly concern. "Nothing's wrong. But the baby just kicked." She took his hands in hers and pressed them against her swollen flesh.

At first Bram thought he imagined the soft stuttering touch against his palm. But a second later, that first kick was followed by a second. Harder. Sharper.

"My God," he breathed, looking at her in stunned amazement. "We really are going to have a baby."

"Yes." Her smile was absolutely beatific. "We really are."

He wanted to stay home with her, but Dani insisted he go to the studio. After all, according to the childbirth classes they'd been attending, the baby's sudden athletic displays were perfectly normal.

Besides, she pointed out, tonight he'd be screening the final cut of *Scandals* for the studio executives and she knew he wanted one last opportunity to look at the film alone before subjecting it to criticism from a group of individuals more interested in the bottom line than telling a good story.

"If you're sure." The baby began turning somersaults. Fascinated, Bram was reluctant to take his hand away.

"Positive." She leaned forward and kissed him. "We'll celebrate tonight. After your successful screening."

"You're that sure it's going to be a success?"

"How could it not?" Her mouth curved against his. "It was, after all, written by the most brilliant writer in Hollywood." Her lips plucked playfully at his. "Not to mention being directed by that world-famous, devastatingly sexy, Oscarwinning director, Bramwell Fortune."

"You're prejudiced."

"Damn right, I am." She grinned at him with wifely pride. "Now, you'd better go. Before I get any more turned on and tie you to this bed and have my wicked way with you."

"Tonight," he promised. "If you're serious about that ty-ing-up stuff, I can bring some handcuffs home from the stu-dio prop department."

She appeared to be considering that. "Will restraints be necessary?"

"To keep me in your bed? Never."

IN THE GRAND AVENUE BAR at Los Angeles's famed Biltmore Hotel, a couple sat at a small table. Their Mies van der Rohe chairs were so close together that their knees were touching beneath the Italian-marble tabletop. The man was drinking an imported German beer from a crystal schooner; the woman was on her third champagne cocktail.

"This is all so exciting," Eden Vail purred, smiling at her companion over the rim of her fluted glass. "And a little un-believable."

"You're a talented actress, Ms. Vail—"

"Eden," she broke in silkily. She took a cigarette from a gold mesh case and placed it between her crimson lips.

"Eden," Peter Bannister corrected, with a warm, obliging smile. He lit the cigarette as expected. "As I told you, Ban-nister Oil and Gas is anxious to expand our investment base. And while movies are reported to be risky, with the right people, we think we can guarantee a good return on our stockholders' money."

"And you think I'm the right person?"

"Eden, believe me, you're the ideal person for the role I have in mind." It was the first true thing he'd said in the last two hours.

"Well, gracious." She exhaled a plume of blue smoke. Her practiced smile was dazzling. It was the one she'd spent years perfecting for the night she'd accept her Oscar. "The idea that you would invest all those millions of dollars in little old me just literally gives me goose bumps.

"See for yourself." She held out a tanned arm for his in-spection. Behind them a gilt-framed painting was illuminated by a soft light that also made her long fingernails gleam like rubies.

On cue, Peter Bannister ran his fingers up the silky, fragrant flesh. Never one to miss an opportunity to leverage her sexual advantage, the actress had arrived at the meeting today in a black jersey micromini halter dress that hugged every lush curve and displayed a great deal of skin. "Perhaps you're just cold."

"They do have the air conditioner turned down awfully low." Her lips pursed around the long slim cigarette as she inhaled. Her emerald eyes met his and held, letting him know that she was more than ready for their business meeting to progress to a more intimate level.

Peter was finding it a pleasant surprise to discover that the Hollywood casting couch actually still existed. Perhaps, after settling things once and for all with the man who'd stolen his wife, he should talk his father into investing in the movies.

"I wouldn't want you to be uncomfortable." He caressed her bare shoulder. "Perhaps we should move this meeting somewhere warmer. Like upstairs." He'd booked the room earlier.

"I think that's a delightful idea." She stabbed the cigarette out in the ashtray. Her smile, her heated, intensely direct gaze, her breathy voice—all promised sensual delights.

As they left the bar together, Peter thought of Dani. And how she was about to discover her folly in thinking she could ever get away from him.

She could run.

But she'd never be able to run fast enough.

Or far enough.

The memory of his wife on her knees, naked, with tears streaming down her face, begging him through bruised, swollen lips not to kill her, made him hard.

Soon, Peter Bannister vowed. Very, very soon.

DANI WAS DRESSING for the screening when the phone rang.

"Sweetheart, it's me."

How was it that even hearing Bram's voice on the phone could make her blood run warmer? Dani wondered. "I'm almost ready."

"That's just it. Something's come up."

She could hear the tension in his voice. "No problem. I'll just drive to the studio myself."

"I don't want you driving in this weather. That road's bad enough without all the rain."

"I grew up driving in blizzards," she reminded him.

"I wasn't in love with you in those days," he told her. "I'm sending a car and driver."

Not wanting to give him any more worries on this all-important night, she merely said, "If it'll make you feel better, fine."

There was a slight pause before Bram answered her. "Terrific." Dani thought he sounded distracted. "See you soon." His voice deepened. "I love you, Mrs. Cantrell."

His husky declaration made her smile. "I love you, too, Mr. Cantrell."

After he'd hung up, Bram turned to the woman who'd just exited the adjoining bathroom. "You have two minutes to get the hell out of here," he said, his voice cold and dangerous. "Or I'm calling security."

Eden Vail appeared unperturbed by his gritty tone. "Whatever you say, lover." She was on her way to the door when she stopped in front of him and planted a hot, deep kiss on his scowling lips. And then she was gone.

Still frowning, Bram dragged the back of his hand across his mouth as if he could wipe away his former lover's taste, and vowed that tomorrow morning he was taking Dani on an overdue honeymoon to some faraway tropical island where life moved at a slower pace and there was nothing for him to do but spend the sun-filled days and star-kissed nights making mad, passionate love to his wife.

Although the limousine arrived twenty minutes early, Dani was already ready. She took one last look in the floor-length mirror and decided the outrageously expensive, tiered, scarlet silk Empire-style evening dress had been worth every penny. The bell rang again. Quickly putting on the ruby earrings Bram had surprised her with just last night, she grabbed her evening bag and a small umbrella. Then she opened the door.

Her heart froze when she discovered Peter Bannister, clad in the navy blue uniform of a limo driver, standing on her porch.

"Hello, sweetheart."

She went to slam the door shut, but he was quicker. He caught hold of the edge of the door and shoved, pushing his way into the house.

Dani wheeled and ran for the phone. But once again he'd anticipated her moves and caught hold of her arm. There was the sound of fabric ripping as he tore her sleeve away from the shoulder seam.

"Not this time, Danielle." His voice was remarkably calm as he took away her beaded purse and her umbrella and tossed them aside. His eyes were not. "This time we're going to play the scene my way." His fingers were cutting off the circulation in her upper arm, but Dani refused to give him the pleasure of seeing her flinch.

Don't panic. Keep him talking, she told herself as she watched in horror when he yanked the phone from the wall. You have to buy time until you can figure a way out of this.

"What scene is that, Peter?" Her knees were shaking, her throat was closing.

"One we've played before," he said matter-of-factly. "But this time, it's going to have a different ending."

Her body was sheathed in ice. But remembering how he'd enjoyed her terror, Dani managed to swallow the hysteria bubbling up in her throat.

"You'd better leave before Bram gets home," she warned in a voice that was remarkably steady. "We have a screening to attend this evening. He'll be here to pick me up at any minute."

"Nice try, sweetheart. But I don't think so." He reached into his jacket pocket and pulled out a manila envelope. "As you'll see, your husband's a little occupied at the moment."

He took some photographs from the envelope and held them out to her.

With nerveless fingers Dani flipped through the Polaroid snapshots. At first glance they appeared horridly incriminating: Bram opening his office door to Eden Vail, Eden in various stages of undress, Eden naked in Bram's arms, her slender arms twined around his neck, her open mouth pressed against his.

There had been a time when she might have actually believed Peter's damning photographs. But no longer. Because during their brief marriage, she'd come to not only love Bram Fortune, but to trust him. Every bit as much as she'd always trusted his younger brother.

Anger rose to take the edge off Dani's fear. "Really, Peter," she said, "if you wanted to break up my marriage, I'd have thought you could come up with something more clever than the old ploy of staging a phony seduction scene."

"Those pictures aren't staged."

"Of course they are." She made a sound of disgust and tossed the photos uncaringly onto the floor.

"Now that's where you're wrong, sweetheart. Because they happen to be every bit as real as these." He reached into his pocket and flashed another batch of photographs. "Why don't you have a look?"

She turned her head, refusing to look. "Go to hell."

"If I do, I'm taking you with me." Furious that she hadn't been fatally wounded by the photos of Eden and Fortune he'd taken earlier that evening, Peter shoved Dani into a nearby chair. "You're going to look at what a slut looks like." Fury raged in his eyes as he threw the new photos into her lap. "Look at them, dammit!"

Reminding herself that the important thing was to escape this nightmare alive, she glanced down with scant interest at the photos, which had been blown up to a riveting eight-by-ten.

As she focused on the top photograph, a shock of recognition shot through her. Her stomach roiled but she bit back the bile that rose in her throat, refusing to give this man the satisfaction of knowing he'd made her ill.

The photographs, obviously taken over the past weeks, revealed Bram and her in a variety of intimate situations. Somehow, Peter had managed to capture them making love—in the bed, the bathtub, even that remarkably heated time in the shower. It sickened her that their privacy had been so invaded, that their lovemaking could be so horridly debased by a man who could never know the meaning of love.

An icy fury flowed over her earlier fear. "You bastard."

"Sticks and stones," he said, with a laugh that held more menace than humor.

Despising him, but unwilling to let him see how he'd so easily tapped into her emotions, Dani forced her expression into one of calm disregard.

"Well, now that we've had our little show-and-tell, I think it's time for you to go, Peter."

A muscle jerked in his cheek. "Oh, I'm going, all right. But I'm not leaving alone."

He leaned over and ran his hand down her cheek. Then her neck. His touch felt like a snake crawling on her skin.

"Don't touch me."

"I'll touch you all I want." The buttons on the scarlet dress were faux rubies surrounded by gold filigree. He popped the first one open with a flick of his thumb and forefinger. "Whenever I want."

Another button followed. "In case you've forgotten, Danielle, a husband has certain inalienable rights to his wife's body."

When those treacherous fingers traced a lethal path along the lace edge of her bra, Dani couldn't withhold a slight, involuntary shiver. "You're not my husband any longer."

"That's what you think." He cupped her sensitive breast in his palm and gave it a hard, vicious squeeze. All the time he was watching her eyes, looking for a sign of the fear and pain he'd always enjoyed.

"I'm going to have you, Dani. In every way there is. And some you never thought possible. And then I'm going to teach you what happens to willful, runaway wives."

He pulled a blue steel pistol from beneath the navy jacket and touched the barrel against her pale cheek in a horrid parody of a caress. The cruel gleam in his eyes told her that he was on the brink of the kind of dangerous frenzy she'd witnessed too many times before. "Let's go."

"Go?" *Stall,* her fevered mind reminded her.

"Your husband called for a car." His voice had regained its earlier calm tone. But Dani could hear the venom in it. "It's outside." His fingers tightened around her upper arm as he yanked her from the chair. The photos scattered across the floor. "Let's go."

Although she dreaded the idea of going anywhere with this man, Dani knew that she'd stand a better chance of getting away outside the house. With that in mind, she swallowed her rising panic and allowed him to lead her out the door to where the long black car was waiting.

Rain streamed over her bare head, destroying the elegant French roll she'd spent nearly an hour creating.

"How did you know about the car?"

"Isn't that obvious? I've had your phone tapped for weeks."

"What did you do to the driver?"

"Nothing. The real driver will be arriving anytime. But you'll already be gone." He laughed at that. "At first I was considering allowing Fortune to come fetch you." His smile turned to a frown. "I rather liked the idea of taking care of both of you at once. Especially after that fiasco at the studio."

Comprehension dawned. "You set the fire."

"Not me. I paid some guy who's supposed to know about such things. Apparently he does a lot of insurance work. Unfortunately, the idiot set the timers wrong. The place was supposed to go up in flames while Fortune was working." He cursed as he dragged her down the stairs. "That's why this time, I decided to finish things myself."

Dani choked down the metallic taste of horror. "Finish things?"

He didn't answer her shaky question. Instead, he stopped and gave her a long look. "Remember the night we met?"

"Not really," she lied.

"It was at that party in Montparnasse. You were wearing red silk, just like you are tonight. God, you looked sexy. Every man in the place wanted you. But you went home with me."

He ran the gun down her throat. Between her breasts. The metal felt cold and deadly against her bare skin. Dani didn't dare talk. It was all she could do to keep from screaming.

"It was raining that night, too. We took a limo home from the party and I made love to you in the back seat while the rain clattered on the car roof and the tinted windows fogged. Remember now?"

She swallowed and nodded. "I felt like a princess," she murmured. Unfortunately, Peter could not have been a more unlikely Prince Charming.

"Do you also remember me telling you that you were mine?"

When she couldn't get the words out, he released her arm to slap her. Hard. "Answer me, dammit!" Another backhanded blow sent her head reeling.

His voice, no longer calm, held a note she'd heard too many times before. He was about to lose it, Dani realized.

"Yes!" she shouted back at him. The rain was streaming down her face, over her shoulders, causing her still-open dress to cling wetly against her rounded body. She was shivering, not from the cold, but from long-repressed fury.

"I remember. I remember everything, dammit!" She also remembered how she'd vowed never to let this man hurt her again. "I remember the hitting and the taunts and the lies. I remember the pain. And most of all, I remember you leaving me for dead. If Ryan hadn't been working at the hospital that night—"

"But he was. And what goes around, comes around."

She pushed the wet hair from her eyes. "What the hell does that mean?"

"It means, my dear unfaithful wife, that your lover's death up on that mountain was not an accident."

No! She sagged against the wooden railing. "I don't believe you."

"It's true. You should have realized I'd never let you marry another man, Dani. I followed you and Fortune to Tahoe City. When I realized your lover was going skiing in the wilderness, I knew fate had handed me a golden opportunity."

"An avalanche killed Ryan."

"Only after I shot at him and missed." Excitement at the memory of what he'd done sharpened Peter's voice.

Dani recalled Bram saying he'd heard a shot just before the mountain exploded. A sound like a tree branch cracking. Or, dear Lord, a rifle shot.

"The report of the rifle started the avalanche," she said flatly. Her stomach and her mind were churning. She felt as if she were going to throw up. Or faint.

"Exactly." His teeth flashed a white, satisfied smile. And then he frowned. "Too bad Mother Nature isn't going to be as cooperative tonight."

"Damn you!" Forgetting the gun, forgetting her fear, forgetting the pain he'd already caused her, forgetting everything except how very much she hated him, Dani began pounding on Peter's chest.

Her furious response caught him off guard. Startled, he lurched back. The railing broke and as he fell backward down the steps, the gun fired. The bullet struck the light fixture above her head, shattering glass and throwing the stairs into darkness. Dani sprinted down the steps, past his sprawled body, and began running. When her high heels bogged down in the sand, she kicked them off, continuing on down the beach in her stocking feet.

She heard the explosion of a shot behind her. Then another, which hit a green metal trash can close by before ricocheting off. But Dani did not look back.

Since it was darker nearer the water, she headed toward the surf, thinking that it would make her a less visible target. The rough sand shredded the feet of her stockings; the cold waves lapped nearly to her knees, soaking the scarlet silk. The rain continued to fall, making her feel as if she were wading through a slanting metal curtain.

She wondered desperately if she'd live to see Bram again. She thought of their child, of the glorious life they'd planned together. Of all the years of love waiting for them.

Another shot sounded. Dani kept running. For her life.

ALTHOUGH HIS MIND should have been on the upcoming screening, all Bram's thoughts were centered on Dani as he drove through the pouring rain to Malibu. At the last minute, he'd canceled the limo, preferring to drive Dani to the studio himself.

When he arrived and saw a black limo parked beside the house, then realized that the porch light—which was on a solar cell—wasn't on, unease rippled through him.

He left the car and took the steps two at a time. The porch light had been shattered. Slivers of glass were strewn all over the deck. The railing was broken and the door was standing wide open. Everything inside Bram went cold and still. Fear sprinted from his stomach to his throat.

"Dani!"

His shout was greeted with ominous, stony silence.

The photos were the first thing Bram saw, scattered over the floor. As he focused on one particularly graphic one of him and Dani in the shower, a red haze covered his eyes.

Although logic told him that anyone could be responsible for this—including that crackpot religious group that had been driving him crazy—Bram knew, deep in his gut, that this was the work of one man.

During his work on *Scandals*, he'd delved deeply into the twisted personalities of overly possessive men who felt the need to control by fear and violence. From Dani's horrific story, he had known that Peter Bannister was that kind of man. Bram managed, with effort, to go to the kitchen phone and call the police. Then he went outside and looked out over the deserted beach, the empty, black ocean.

Where the hell were they?

Desperate to find Dani, to save her, Bram was forced to accept the unholy truth that there was nothing he could do but wait for the police to arrive.

And then what? he asked himself.

His hands curled into fists. His mouth was a harsh grim line as the answer came. *I'll kill him.*

IN THE DISTANCE, she could hear a dog bark. Closer still, she could hear Peter's footfalls thudding on the tide-hardened sand.

She was nearing an outcropping of rocks. Familiar with the beach from her nightly walks with Bram, Dani turned inland, headed to the stairs she knew would be there.

The dry sand was thick and sluggish again. Her breathing was ragged and her heart was burning. But fear had created an adrenaline rush that drove everything from her mind but the urge to flee.

Risking a glance back over her shoulder, she saw Peter stumble. When he began screaming and cursing and digging in the sand, she guessed he'd dropped the gun.

Her heart was pounding painfully against her ribs, hurting each time it beat as she grasped hold of the metal railing and practically pulled herself up the steep stone steps leading to the top of the cliff.

She slipped once, falling to her knees, scraping her skin on the rough rocks. Her dress clung to her, cold and clammy. She pressed her palms against her stomach.

"Don't worry," she assured her baby. "Nothing's going to happen. Mama's not going to let anyone hurt you."

Close by, she heard the steady hum of traffic on the coast road.

The nearly deserted highway was well lit. And blessedly inviting. Heading toward it, she tried to call out for help. But with her lungs burning so horribly, she couldn't run and breathe at the same time.

When another shot shattered the night, she realized that Peter had found the gun. Although he'd already proved himself no marksman, it was, she feared, only a matter of time.

Finally Dani saw the highway. Lifting her heavy wet skirts higher, she caught a second wind and sprinted toward it.

THE L.A. COUNTY Sheriff Department descended on Bram's beach house within less than three minutes of his call. In this land where image was everything, they seemed determined that the story that would be played out tomorrow morning in the worldwide press would end successfully.

Several deputies took to the beach. Others to the street. A bulletin was broadcast all over the county, advising to be on the lookout for Bannister's car.

Bram was riding shotgun in one of the patrol cars with a deputy who, in a misguided attempt to reassure his passenger, was regaling him with stories of other local crimes.

He'd just finished a tawdry tale about a serial rapist when a woman suddenly burst from the darkness, appearing like an wild apparition in the yellow beam of the headlights.

The deputy slammed on the brakes. Tires squealed, but fortunately, the car did not skid on the wet pavement.

Heedless of the drenching rain, Bram was out of the car like a shot.

Seconds later, a very wet and very terrified Dani flung herself into his arms.

Right behind her came Bannister, every bit as wet as Dani and waving a deadly looking pistol.

The deputy pulled out his own automatic weapon. "Put the gun down, Mr. Bannister," he warned. "It's all over."

"The hell it is!" Peter shouted. "The slut has to pay!" Obsessed with his plan to punish Dani for imagined sins, he got off yet another wild shot that struck the windshield of the patrol car.

The deputy, having no choice, returned fire.

And then there was only silence. And the soft, steady sound of falling rain.

Epilogue

IT WAS LIKE A SCENE from Currier and Ives. Outside the cabin, fat white snowflakes floated down from the sky, turning the forest into a winter wonderland. Inside, a red-and-orange fire crackled in the grate and a dark green pine wreath studded with pinecones and bright crimson holly and adorned with a red velvet ribbon, hung on the door. Three red-and-white stockings were hanging from the mantel, and above it was a family portrait painted by Dani.

A wooden crèche, which had been hand carved by some distant ancestor and handed down to five succeeding generations of Fortunes so far, claimed space beneath the Christmas tree.

The spicy fragrance of the towering blue spruce mingled enticingly with the aroma of burning cedar and baking gingerbread. Christmas carols played on the CD.

An easel in the corner displayed Dani's latest work in progress. Her painting, during her marriage to Bram, had evolved. While they still concentrated on surprise twists, the surprises were no longer dark and terrifying. This latest series, for example, depicted ethereal winged angels playing various mortal roles—fire fighters, police officers, teachers, librarians, mothers and fathers.

Dani was sitting on the sofa in front of the fire, her feet up on the coffee table, gazing with quiet contentment at the tree it had taken five days to locate in the woods behind the cabin and two additional days to trim. Decorated with an eclectic selection of antique glass balls, hand-painted ornaments she'd made herself and primitive angels created by two-year-old Hannah Fortune from construction paper, yarn, glue and glitter, the tree was like everything else in Dani's life these days.

Absolutely perfect.

Bram stood in the doorway, two mugs of eggnog in his hands, and allowed himself the pure pleasure of drinking in the sight of his wife. This would be their third Christmas together, and each year, as impossible as it seemed, only got better.

There were times—and this was one of them—when he couldn't believe that he'd been so blessed. He had, hands down, the most beautiful, talented wife in the world. As for Hannah, their dark-haired, gypsy-eyed daughter, friends and acquaintances alike had learned the hard way that merely asking about Bram Fortune's child inevitably resulted in a long discussion regarding her latest artistic endeavor, followed by the latest batch of photographs.

"I'm not promising anything," he murmured as he sank down beside her, "but I think she's finally going to stay asleep."

Dani smiled up at her husband as she took the mug he held out to her. "Aren't you clever."

"Don't give me the credit." He put his arm around her shoulder. "I think it was the sixth reading of the Grinch that finally did it."

"Christmas Eve is an exciting night for children," Dani reminded him.

Still unable to resist the creamy lure of her skin, Bram nibbled lightly on her neck. "For grown-ups, too." He reached behind a pillow and pulled out a gold-wrapped box. "I thought, since things are bound to be wild tomorrow, after Santa's visit and with Mom and Dad coming over for breakfast, we might exchange one present each, tonight."

"What a lovely idea." She touched her smiling lips to his. "And as it happens, one I happened to have myself." She took her own wrapped gift from behind the pillow at her end of the sofa.

"Great minds." Bram recaptured her lips, cupping the back of her neck so he could linger over the kiss. "Have I told you lately that I'm crazy about you?"

"Just this morning." She sighed happily as his clever lips moved on to warm the vulnerable hollow of her throat. "But feel free to tell me again."

He nudged the cowl neck of her sweater aside and nuzzled her neck. Her shoulder. "I'm crazy about you, Mrs. Fortune."

"That's nice." How easily he could make her giddy, Dani thought, as her blood warmed and the mists began floating over her mind again. Even after all this time. "Since I'm pretty crazy about you, too, Mr. Fortune."

Her eyes were lit with an irresistible mixture of amusement and desire. It was a look that never failed to seduce.

"Aren't you going to open your present?" He'd been going crazy all day, envisioning her in his gift.

To love, and to be loved in return, Dani considered, as she slipped the silver ribbon from the box. Now that was surely the most wonderful gift of all.

"Oh, Bram." She drew in a breath at the exquisite ivory satin confection. The clingy nightgown reminded her of something Jean Harlow might have worn. She liked the idea that Bram still found her sexy after more than three years of shared domesticity. "It's stunning."

"Not as stunning as the lady I bought it for."

She kissed him. "I'll wear it tonight."

He kissed her back. "That's exactly what I was hoping you'd say."

Practically bursting with having kept her gift a secret this long, Dani handed him the flat package. "Your turn."

It took a moment to sink in. Bram stared down at the opened gift. "Is this what I think it is?"

"A sonogram." Her pleased, female smile rivaled the Mona Lisa's. "Of our child."

"Hannah?" He turned it, trying a different angle.

"No." The smile touched her eyes. "Not Hannah."

His startled gaze went from the black-and-white ultrasound image to Dani's face. "Are you saying—?"

"There will be two children wanting you to read the Grinch to them next Christmas."

"When?"

"Late June."

"June." He looked back down at the sonogram, then back at Dani. "Thank you."

She laughed at that—a bright, musical sound Bram knew would have the power to thrill him when they were in their nineties.

"You don't have to thank me, darling." She linked her hands around his neck and sank into his deep warm kiss. "After all, I certainly didn't do it alone."

"Speaking of which—" he stood, pulling her with him "—this definitely calls for a celebration." He scooped her up in his arms, grabbed the nightgown and headed up the stairs.

"What about Hannah's dollhouse?" The three-story Victorian house was still in its box, waiting to be put together.

"You happen to be married to an intelligent, clever man," he reminded her as they entered the bedroom.

"I realize that. Still—"

He smothered her worried argument with his lips as he lowered her to her feet on the plank floor. "Besides," he continued, after they came up for air, "we've got all night."

"Most of the night," she reminded him silkily. She plucked the nightgown from his hand and went into the adjoining bathroom to put it on.

"It's just a dollhouse," he called in to her as he undressed on the other side of the door. "How hard could it be to put a kid's toy together?"

The nightgown slipped over her body like a satin waterfall. "How hard, indeed?" she agreed as she rejoined him.

Holding her arms out to her sides—like Hannah showing off the new red velvet Christmas dress her grandparents had bought her—Dani turned around. Cut in a deep vee in front and plunging below the waist in back, the long, sleek shimmer of ivory satin hugged her feminine curves like a lover's caress. It was also as sexy as sin.

Looking at her, captured in a slash of moonlight every bit as white and seductive as the gown, Bram gave thanks to nameless gods for sending this goddess to him.

He drew her into his arms. Her skin was every bit as soft as the satin and smelled like heaven in the springtime.

"I've got an idea," he murmured against her mouth.

The whisper of his fingertips at the small of her back warmed. The devils in his dark eyes excited.

Was there a woman alive who didn't dream of her man looking at her with such hot, avid hunger? Dani wondered. She twined her arms around his neck and surrendered to the wildly primitive urges beating in her blood. To the rhythm he could still stir so easily, with only a look. Or a touch.

"I'm always open to new ideas."

"Why don't we just tell Hannah that Santa's elves went on strike?" He nudged one satin strap off a creamy shoulder with his teeth. "That way, Dad can help me put the dollhouse together tomorrow morning."

Dani's answering laugh, as Bram eased her back against the pillows, was free and breezy.

"Oh, I do so love being married to an intelligent, clever man!"

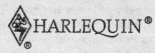

HARLEQUIN®

Weddings, Inc.

THE VENGEFUL GROOM
Sara Wood

Legend has it that those married in Eternity's
chapel are destined for a lifetime of happiness.
But happiness isn't what Giovanni wants from
marriage—it's revenge!

Ten years ago, Tina's testimony sent Gio to
prison—for a crime he didn't commit. *Now* he's
back in Eternity and looking for a bride. *Now*
Tina is about to learn just how ruthless and
disturbingly sensual Gio's brand of vengeance
can be.

THE VENGEFUL GROOM, available in
October from Harlequin Presents, is the fifth
book in Harlequin's new cross-line series,
WEDDINGS, INC. Be sure to look for
the sixth book, **EDGE OF ETERNITY,** by
Jasmine Cresswell (Harlequin Intrigue #298),
coming in November.

WED5

HARLEQUIN®

Don't miss these Harlequin favorites by some of our most distinguished authors!
And now you can receive a discount by ordering two or more titles!

HT #25525	THE PERFECT HUSBAND by Kristine Rolofson	$2.99	☐
HT #25554	LOVERS' SECRETS by Glenda Sanders	$2.99	☐
HP #11577	THE STONE PRINCESS by Robyn Donald	$2.99	☐
HP #11554	SECRET ADMIRER by Susan Napier	$2.99	☐
HR #03277	THE LADY AND THE TOMCAT by Bethany Campbell	$2.99	☐
HR #03283	FOREIGN AFFAIR by Eva Rutland	$2.99	☐
HS #70529	KEEPING CHRISTMAS by Marisa Carroll	$3.39	☐
HS #70578	THE LAST BUCCANEER by Lynn Erickson	$3.50	☐
HI #22256	THRICE FAMILIAR by Caroline Burnes	$2.99	☐
HI #22238	PRESUMED GUILTY by Tess Gerritsen	$2.99	☐
HAR #16496	OH, YOU BEAUTIFUL DOLL by Judith Arnold	$3.50	☐
HAR #16510	WED AGAIN by Elda Minger	$3.50	☐
HH #28719	RACHEL by Lynda Trent	$3.99	☐
HH #28795	PIECES OF SKY by Marianne Willman	$3.99	☐

Harlequin Promotional Titles

#97122	LINGERING SHADOWS by Penny Jordan	$5.99	☐
	(limited quantities available on certain titles)		

	AMOUNT	$	
DEDUCT:	**10% DISCOUNT FOR 2+ BOOKS**	$	
	POSTAGE & HANDLING	$	
	($1.00 for one book, 50¢ for each additional)		
	APPLICABLE TAXES*	$ _____	
	TOTAL PAYABLE	$ _____	
	(check or money order—please do not send cash)		

To order, complete this form and send it, along with a check or money order for the total above, payable to Harlequin Books, to: **In the U.S.:** 3010 Walden Avenue, P.O. Box 9047, Buffalo, NY 14269-9047; **In Canada:** P.O. Box 613, Fort Erie, Ontario, L2A 5X3.

Name: _____

Address: _____City: _____

State/Prov.: _____ Zip/Postal Code: _____

*New York residents remit applicable sales taxes.
 Canadian residents remit applicable GST and provincial taxes..

HBACK-JS

Bestselling Temptation author Elise Title is back with a funny, sexy trilogy—THE HART GIRLS—written in the vein of her popular miniseries THE FORTUNE BOYS!

Rachel, Julie and Kate Hart are three women of the nineties with heart and spark. They're determined to win the TV ratings wars—and win the men of their dreams!

Stay tuned for:

#509 DANGEROUS AT HEART (October 1994)
#513 HEARTSTRUCK (November 1994)
#517 HEART TO HEART (December 1994)

Available wherever Harlequin books are sold.

This September, discover the fun of falling in love with...

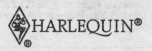

Harlequin is pleased to bring you this exciting new collection of three original short stories by bestselling authors!

ELISE TITLE
BARBARA BRETTON
LASS SMALL

LOVE AND LAUGHTER—sexy, romantic, fun stories guaranteed to tickle your funny bone and fuel your fantasies!

Available in September wherever Harlequin books are sold.

◆ HARLEQUIN®

RIGHT MAN...WRONG TIME

Remember that one man who turned your world upside down? Who made you experience all the ecstatic highs of passion and lows of loss and regret. What if you met him again?

If you missed any Lost Loves titles, here's your chance to order them:

Harlequin Temptation®—Lost Loves

#25589	THE RETURN OF CAINE O'HALLORAN by JoAnn Ross	$2.99	☐
#25593	WHAT MIGHT HAVE BEEN by Glenda Sanders	$2.99 U.S. $3.50 CAN.	☐ ☐
#25600	FORMS OF LOVE by Rita Clay Estrada	$2.99 U.S. $3.50 CAN.	☐ ☐
#25601	GOLD AND GLITTER by Gina Wilkins	$2.99 U.S. $3.50 CAN.	☐ ☐
#25605	EVEN COWBOYS GET THE BLUES by Carin Rafferty	$2.99 U.S. $3.50 CAN.	☐ ☐
	(limited quantities available on certain titles)		

TOTAL AMOUNT	$
POSTAGE & HANDLING	$
($1.00 for one book, 50¢ for each additional)	
APPLICABLE TAXES*	$_____
TOTAL PAYABLE	$_____
(check or money order—please do not send cash)	

To order, complete this form and send it, along with a check or money order for the total above, payable to Harlequin Books, to: **In the U.S.:** 3010 Walden Avenue, P.O. Box 9047, Buffalo, NY 14269-9047; **In Canada:** P.O. Box 613, Fort Erie, Ontario, L2A 5X3.

Name: _____

Address: _____ City: _____

State/Prov.: _____ Zip/Postal Code: _____

*New York residents remit applicable sales taxes.
Canadian residents remit applicable GST and provincial taxes.